KISSED

KISSED

C.J. SHANE

Published by Rope's End Publishing
P.O. Box 13689, Tucson, AZ 85732
www.RopesEndPublishing.com

hardcover: 978-1-951524-02-9
paperback: 978-1-951524-03-6
epub: 978-1-951524-04-3
Kindle mobi: 978-1-951524-05-0

Typesetting services by BOOKOW.COM

For all the living creatures of the Borderlands: saguaro and hawk, rattlesnake and coyote, jaguar and ocotillo, and the people, too, both Mexican and American

Acknowledgments

Sincere thanks go to Diane C. Taylor for making this story coherent and readable, to Dawn in County Durham for making Miles sound like a real Englishman, to Bookow for excellent formatting, to my ARC team for reading and reviewing, and to Destiny Hawkins at Vibrant Designs for the excellent cover.

Letty Valdez Mysteries

Desert Jade 2017

Dragon's Revenge 2018

Daemon Waters 2019

Cat Miranda Mysteries

Kissed 2020

CONTENTS

1 THE INTRUDER

Cat Miranda's eyes opened suddenly. A noise. Downstairs. Then silence. Maybe she had imagined it? No, there it was again.

She held still in her bed, almost not breathing. Her heart began to hammer in her chest. She could hear the sound of a key or something metal being thrust into her backdoor lock and jiggled noisily.

Someone was breaking into her home and her art gallery! Cat could barely control her trembling and shallow breath. She sat up, and looked at her bedside clock. Midnight. She'd been asleep an hour or so.

What the hell? She'd only been back in Bisbee for two days. She had been almost overwhelmed with exhaustion after driving nearly four hours from Phoenix, then hauling her luggage and a couple of boxes into the living quarters above the art gallery. That was tiring enough, but she was also struggling to manage all the things that her new life would bring her. That included opening the gallery again. Meanwhile, she was dealing with intense grief over the death of her brother. It was almost more than she could handle. She frequently found herself in tears.

And now a break-in? Too much! She fought back tears and struggled to control her fear. She had to deal with this and deal with it now. She threw the bed covers back, slipped out of bed and crept to her bedroom door. Now she could hear the door downstairs opening and the sounds of someone entering her house. Oh god. What to do? She was filled with alarm.

Cat reached for the baseball bat she kept nearby in the corner of her room. She silently opened her bedroom door and crept onto the landing at the top of the stairs. There were two light switches on the wall, one for a light behind and over her head, and one in the ceiling directly above the back door. She flipped on the light above the back door as she stood still in the darkness of the landing. At the same time, she lifted the baseball bat in her two hands.

The light coming on revealed a man standing inside her house at the open back door. He was shrugging off a backpack, and at the same time, pulling a small suitcase on rollers into her house. He stopped when the light suddenly came on. He looked around, eyes squinted.

"*Merde*," he muttered in an irritated voice.

"What the hell are you doing breaking into my house?" Cat said loudly. She tried to control the trembling in her voice. She was scared, but she didn't want the intruder to know it.

The man looked up at her, seeing her for the first time. He was still squinting, trying to adjust to the sudden bright light in his eyes.

"I'm not breaking in. I have a key," he said roughly. He held up the key in his hand.

"You have an accent," Cat blurted out.

"I can't help that. I'm English," he growled.

"Okay, smart ass. Where did you get a key to my house? And why are you here?"

"I rented a room in this place for two weeks from a chap named Luis Miranda. He gave me the key. Where is he? And who the hell are you?" The man was obviously irritated. His eyes were open now and staring at her. He was scowling.

Cat felt a pain in her chest at the mention of Luis, a pain in her heart.

"I'm Cat Miranda. Luis was my brother."

"*Was?* What do you mean *was?*"

"Luis died nearly a month ago."

The man's voice changed. "Oh, I'm sorry." His tone was completely different now. He sounded genuinely sympathetic. "What happened? Was there an accident?"

"No, he was really sick. He never got better. I took care of him until the end."

"I am very sorry. I arranged this rental about six months ago. I didn't know he was ill."

"What are you doing here?"

"I'm a visiting scholar doing research. I'm close to the end of my journey so I'll be going home in a couple of weeks. I decided to spend my last days in this lovely little town near the border."

"Oh." That made sense. Cat agreed with him that her childhood home, Bisbee, Arizona, was indeed a lovely little town in the Mule Mountains of southern Arizona. The international border at Naco was only a few miles away. Bisbee had been a mining town for a long time, but now the Copper Queen Mine was open only for tours. Bisbee had become an arts and music destination.

She made a sudden decision the way she usually made them. Hers was a spontaneous, gut decision based on intuition. He seemed okay. If this guy was telling the truth, and he seemed to be, Luis had trusted him. If Luis trusted him, then Cat could trust him. Cat decided to let him in, just hoping she wouldn't regret it later. She'd keep an eye on him just in case.

"You wait there. I'll be right down."

"As you wish, m'lady."

M'lady. Well, she'd never been called that before, Cat thought.

The man stuck the key in his pocket and began rubbing his eyes with one hand. She thought he looked tired.

Cat disappeared into her bedroom and came out in seconds with a long-sleeve t-shirt pulled over her gown. She had clogs on her feet, too, as she came down the stairs. Gesturing to the man to enter the kitchen before her, she turned on the kitchen light. The baseball bat was still in Cat's hand.

"You behave yourself or else," she said.

"You'll find that I am a really nice bloke, and my behavior is exemplary."

"Bloke," she repeated, shaking her head. "Sit down. Do you want something to drink? You can explain why you're here."

"Hot tea would be welcome." He sat down at the small kitchen table.

Cat put the pot on the stove to heat water. "I don't have any of that English black tea. Will you drink tea that relaxes you and reduces tension?"

"Yes. It seems that we could both benefit from a reduction in tension."

"So who are you? What's this about being a scholar? And tell me about renting a room here." Cat looked the man over. He was tall, slim, and maybe about thirty years old. He had ruffled strawberry blond hair, and there was a little stubble on his face, as if he hadn't shaved for a day or two. His eyes were blue. Very blue. And he was handsome. Yeah, *muy guapo*, she thought to herself.

"My name is Miles Trevelyan. I'm from Sussex. That's on the south coast of England. I've been living in Oxford for several years. When I return home, I'm going to be conducting some seminars at the University of Exeter in Devon next month. I'll be working on a book, too."

"So you came to the U.S. to do research? What are you studying?"

Miles nodded. "The Borderlands. I started in the Rio Grande Valley in Texas and worked my way west all the way to San Diego. I went back and forth across the border as I progressed. I conducted a lot of interviews and took many photos as well as collecting documents. I stopped in here briefly on my way west. I liked Bisbee so much that I decided it would be a great place to decompress before going home. I thought I could start organizing material for my book here, too. Do you have Wi-Fi here? I forgot to ask your brother."

"Yes. We have Wi-Fi."

The water in the pot was hot now. Cat retrieved two cups, put a tea bag in each and filled each cup with hot water. She placed a cup in front of Miles Trevelyan. She sat down at the table across from Miles, put a cup on the table in front of her and a saucer between them for the tea bags. She handed him a spoon.

"Your name is Cat?"

"Catalina Amalia Miranda. You can call me Cat."

"That's a very pretty name. Your brother spoke about you."

"He did?" Cat felt that pain in her heart again.

"Yes. Luis told me he has….had a very sweet baby sister. He said he hoped I would get a chance to meet her…you." Miles's voice was gentle.

Cat's eyes filled with tears. She nodded.

"I came through here and spent the night at the Copper Queen Hotel. I asked around about long-term rentals. It seems that someone knew someone who knew someone who had been talking to Luis. The person I talked to said he thought Luis was considering renting out a room as a trial B&B. So I showed up here. The gallery was open so I looked around while he was talking to some customers. He sold a small painting to them. Then he and I talked about me renting his extra room for a brief time before I return home."

"He never told me."

"If he was ill, he probably had other things on his mind."

Cat nodded. "Luis had pancreatic cancer. He'd had the symptoms for some time. Persistent pain in his stomach, fatigue, weight loss. He ignored it. He was happy running the gallery, and I think he wanted to think about all his upcoming projects, not about being ill. But finally the pain got bad enough that he went to the doctor. He was diagnosed, but even with treatment, it was too late. About a month ago, I came back to Bisbee and took care of him. That way he didn't have to go to hospice. He could die at home."

Miles nodded. He frowned slightly. "Sad."

"So I guess he made those arrangements with you several weeks before he became so ill?"

"Yes, I think you must be right about that."

"I have been living and working in Phoenix since I finished college. I came back home to Bisbee frequently. Luis and I had some heart-to-heart talks on those visits. He and I decided together that we'd be co-owners of the gallery and that I would move back here and run the gallery with him. Then he became ill. When he was sick, he never spoke about death. I realize now that he knew he was dying. He was doing what he always did. He was taking care of his little sister and helping me have a better life."

"You don't think you'll miss Phoenix?"

"No. My life will be better here."

"What kind of work did you do in Phoenix?"

"I'm a graphic designer. I design stuff for businesses like logos and promotional material, advertisements and all that. Also I designed a lot of websites for businesses. I designed our gallery's website, too."

He nodded.

"I'm not really a big city girl," Cat continued. "Phoenix is big. And it's really a lot hotter in the summer than it is in Bisbee." She didn't mention that she also was escaping what she thought of as "man trouble" in the form of her ex-husband.

"Yes, Bisbee is a mile high. Much higher elevation so you have cooler temperatures."

"That's right. So, anyway, after he died, I returned to Phoenix for nearly a month. I had to quit my job and clean out my apartment so I could move back home. Luis had dreams for the gallery. He gave those dreams to me, and now they are my dreams, too. I'm going to try to make them come true."

Miles sipped his tea. "This is surprisingly good tea," he said.

"It's Mexican *manzanilla* tea. Or they call it 'chamomile' in English. Maybe it will help you to sleep better."

"Speaking of which, any suggestions where I could sleep tonight? Know of any cheap hotels or motels?"

Cat paused and stared at her cup of tea. She knew that this weekend was an especially busy one in Bisbee. There was a music festival going on for two days so she knew all the town's hotels and B&Bs were full. He'd probably have to drive twenty miles to the town of Sierra Vista to find a motel. Or go across the border into Mexico and look for a hotel. It was late at night, and that would make the search more difficult.

"Oh, all right. You can stay here," Cat said. She looked at him and said sternly. "I think you are probably okay. I've decided to trust you."

"Good decision. Like I said…."

"Yeah, I know. You're a nice bloke. Okay. Just behave yourself. I've had it up to here with obnoxious men."

"I'll be on my best behavior, m'lady. I promise." He smiled again.

Cat put the two cups in the kitchen sink. "Come on with me, and I'll show you to your room."

Miles followed her up the stairs, bringing his backpack and luggage with him.

At the top of the stairs, Cat opened the door to the room opposite hers. She turned on the light.

"This is Luis's old room. You don't mind sleeping in a room where someone died, do you?"

"No, not at all. This happens a lot in England anyway. We're an old country, and lots of people have died here and there."

So Miles Trevelyan was a smart ass with a peculiar sense of humor, Cat thought to herself.

"Let's get some sleep now, and we'll talk in the morning. Sorry about all the confusion."

"Thank you for allowing me to stay. Good night, m'lady."

Cat went downstairs and checked to make sure the back door was locked. She returned to her room and closed the door. Just to be sure, she jammed the back of a wooden chair under her door knob. She went back to bed feeling even more exhausted than before.

* * *

This time Cat was awakened by sounds that were much louder and much nearer. She opened her eyes and sat up in bed. She glanced at the clock. Three in the morning. She could hear thumping and a crash. Then she heard what sounded like Miles Trevelyan yelling at someone.

"Get out! Now!"

There was no response to his yelling, but the sounds of a struggle continued for a few more seconds. Suddenly everything went quiet.

Cat opened the door to her room, baseball bat in hand.

"Mr. Trevelyan?"

The door to Luis's room flew open. Miles was standing there in a t-shirt and pajama pants, bare-footed.

"Look at this. Hurry."

He stepped aside and pointed to the open floor-to-ceiling glass door on the other side of the room. It led out onto a deck with a stairway that went to the ground floor. The screen on the door had been ripped off.

Cat hurried to the open doorway and looked down. Miles was right behind her. She could see a form dressed in dark clothing running away down the street from her house toward the main road of Tombstone Canyon.

"Oh my god," Cat whispered.

"You had an intruder. Has this happened before?"

"No," Cat said. "Never. We've never had a break-in downstairs either."

Miles turned on a lamp, and a soft light flooded the room. He reached over and put a chair upright that had been knocked over in the struggle.

"I had the glass door open so I could enjoy the cool night air. I sleep better when it's cool. Then I woke when I heard him trying to get the screen door open. I jumped up just as he came into the room. He rushed me and we struggled. He knocked over the chair. I yelled at him, and he backed up, turned and ran away."

"It was a man?"

"Yes, maybe a little heavier built than I am. Maybe not quite as tall as me but almost."

"Are you okay?" Cat looked at Miles. The lamp light revealed a dark mark above one of his eyes.

Miles reached up and touched the spot. He grimaced. "I guess he hit me. Ouch." He looked at his fingers that had just touched the wound. "There's blood."

"Come with me, and let me take a look at you."

She led him to the bathroom which opened onto the landing between her room and Miles's room. She turned on the light in the bathroom.

"Here. Sit down on the toilet seat."

Miles followed her instructions. He sat quietly with his hands on his knees.

Cat bent over to take a look. "Yes, looks like a small cut. Not deep. It's not bleeding anymore. Let me clean it up and put a little bandage on it." She turned and reached into the cabinet over the sink to retrieve hydrogen peroxide and a box of bandage strips.

She gathered some tissue into a wad and began cleaning the cut with hydrogen peroxide. She carefully placed the bandage strip over the cut. She stood back and looked at his forehead.

"Does it hurt?"

"No, not really." He was grinning.

"Why are you smiling?"

"The life of a scholar can be pretty quiet and uneventful. My trip has gone well. No problems at all. Now here at the end of the trip, I've had a chance to fight off a bandito. This little incident will make a great story to tell to my mates at the pub over some beers."

"Bandito?" Cat shook her head. "We're not in Mexico."

"Almost Mexico."

"Okay. Whatever. I'm glad you're happy. I'm not."

"No, I guess not." He looked up at her.

"I don't know why someone tried to break in here. I don't know what they want. This is making me nervous," she paused. "Also, I feel bad for you."

"For me?"

"Yes, you think you are renting a quiet room in a quiet home in a quiet town so you can wind down before you go home. The first thing that happens is an intruder breaks into your room, you get in a struggle, and you get hurt. I'm not being a very good host, am I?"

Miles shrugged. "Don't worry about it. How about if we go back to bed and get some sleep? We can talk about this over breakfast. Maybe we can figure out what's happened here so it won't happen again. Okay?" He stood up.

"You're so calm. I'm a wreck. I don't want to cry. I cry too much these days. I'm too emotional."

"You're doing quite well, Cat, considering all that's happened. Seems that you've just had too much to deal with lately. I'm one of the things you've had to deal with, and I'm very sorry about that. You go to bed now. Close your eyes and take deep, slow breaths in and out. Think about clouds drifting slowly through the sky. You'll be asleep in a few minutes."

"Clouds? Seriously?"

"Seriously. Don't forget the breathing part."

"Okay."

As they left the bathroom, Miles clicked off the light.

Cat went into her room and turned back to him just before she closed the door.

"Clouds?"

"Clouds. Don't forget the slow, rhythmic breathing. The clouds will start singing if you breathe properly. And call me Miles, not Mr. Trevelyan. Okay?"

Cat smiled. "Okay. See you in the morning." She closed the door and returned to her bed. She didn't bother jamming the chair against her door.

Things went just as Miles had said. She closed her eyes and purposefully put thoughts of the intruder out of her mind. She began the slow breathing in and out and imagined clouds floating over the Mule Mountains of Bisbee, Arizona. She drifted off before the clouds had a chance to start singing.

* * *

Miles, on the other hand, was wide awake. After half an hour of staring at the ceiling, he turned on a small lamp, opened his laptop and wrote an email to his dad in Sussex.

Hi Dad, Just wanted you to know that I arrived safely in Bisbee, Arizona. You can find it on the map. It's a small town southeast of Tucson and really close to the U.S.-Mexico border. Very charming little town. You'd like it. Something about it reminds me of Cornwall, but with desert mountains, not the sea. That probably doesn't make any sense, does it? The weather here is great. Very sunny and warm. It's late now so I'll write more tomorrow. Love, Miles

Miles went back to bed. He wasn't any closer to sleep. His state of mind was a combination of excitement and concern. La señorita Catalina Amalia Miranda was the loveliest woman he'd met on this trip. Actually, she was one of the loveliest women he'd ever met anywhere. She wasn't really a conventional beauty, nor would she stand out in a crowd. She was so little that she'd never make it as one of those tall models he saw on television striding down the fashion runway in London. She would, however, fit right under his chin.

Yes, she was lovely. So Mexican. So American. So Borderlands. Yes, that was it. She was a womanly epitome of the Borderlands. Dark eyes. Lovely long dark hair. Rich soft brown skin. Full, soft red lips. Sweet, funny, and very sexy. She seemed completely unaware of her allure. Sitting in front of her in the bathroom when she tended his wound had been a delight. True, he found it amusing to think about scaring off a bandito. But the real delight was Cat herself. She had on a thin nightgown, and his eyes were on the level of her breasts as she cleaned and bandaged his scratch. Yes, delightful. But he'd kept his hands to himself, and he'd said nothing because he had promised her that he'd be a good bloke. He sighed.

Coupled with these pleasant thoughts, Miles also felt a deep concern. Why was someone breaking into Cat's home in the middle of the night? Miles was so glad he'd been there. Otherwise, she would have been all on her own to face the intruder. He would talk to her in the morning to see if they could figure out what they could do to prevent this from happening again. He most definitely wanted the lovely Cat Miranda to be safe.

Miles decided to try the breathing exercises that he'd recommended to Cat. Eventually, he, too, fell asleep.

2 Miles

As usual, Cat woke up at first light. A friend had teased her once and said she must be the child of peasant farmers to wake up so early. She had no idea if she was descended from farmers. She knew only about her mother's family. Her mother came from a long line of hardworking Mexicans and Mexican Americans. They tended shops and worked on cars and cooked meals and ran cattle and sold things in the market. Cat's mom was first in the family to go to college, graduate and then become a nurse. But Cat knew almost nothing about her father.

She stretched out in bed and listened to morning sounds. The house was quiet though she could hear a bird in the mesquite tree near her window. The song sounded like a phainopepla, a type of flycatcher that looked very much like a cardinal but black, not red. She could hear Inca doves, too. No sounds came from Luis's room. Her guest – she frowned slightly at the idea of Miles Trevelyan as a B&B guest – must still be asleep. She didn't really know what to do about his presence. He seemed nice enough, and he was nice to look at. But she had plenty to deal with right now, and a guest was a bit much. Time to rise and shine. She jumped out of bed and went to the bathroom.

Cat looked in the bathroom mirror. She noticed dark shadows under her brown eyes, and her shoulder-length dark hair was a mess. She looked tired and stressed already, and it was only early morning. She sighed, tied her hair with a band and pinned it up. She stepped into the shower. The warm water felt great. After her shower, she dressed in her favorite winter outfit, black leggings, a t-shirt, and a thigh-length, knitted pull-over sweater in a rich magenta color. Her favorite black half-boots went on her feet.

Fifteen minutes later, Cat was downstairs in her tiny kitchen making coffee. She could hear stirring upstairs. While she waited for the coffee, she wandered from the back of the building, where the kitchen was located, to the art gallery in the main part of the building. The gallery had been created by Luis from a large, two-story house that had existed on the property for nearly eighty years. He had hollowed out most of the ground-floor living and dining area to make as large a gallery space as possible. There was a smaller room off the main gallery that he used for storage. The back of the old home still had the tiny kitchen with a small table only big enough for two or three people to sit and eat. Out the back door, the door Miles had entered the previous night, there was a *portál*, an attached covered porch that ran the length of the back of the house. A larger table and several chairs were there ready if she wanted to entertain guests. There was also an old wooden swing on a stand under the porch, too. She and Luis used to sit on it together and take turns reading to each other.

The thought crossed Cat's mind that, if she really wanted to turn the upstairs into a B&B, she was going to have to do some serious remodeling and probably build onto the old structure. But really, there just wasn't enough room for her to live here and have a B&B, too. She wondered what Luis had in mind when he considered opening a B&B. The idea was overwhelming, but then it seemed to Cat that nearly everything was overwhelming these days. Caring for her dying brother, escaping Phoenix, escaping her ex-husband Al, starting a new life here in her childhood home of Bisbee. It was a lot. The idea of a B&B seemed too much right now. Maybe there was something else going on that she didn't know about. But she would never know now what Luis had been thinking because he wasn't here to tell her. Miles Trevelyan seemed like a nice guy, but he was a real inconvenience at the moment.

And there was that second intruder last night. She cringed. Something else to worry about.

She walked slowly around the perimeter of the gallery, the Sonoran Art Gallery. She liked the name. It was a cross-border kind of name that reflected the Sonoran Desert region she lived in. She knew that Luis had a dream of building Bisbee into an art center on the level of Santa Fe, New Mexico. He wanted to give local artists in the Bisbee area a chance to show and sell their art. He hoped to bring artists in from across the border, too. His dream was to make it a real Borderlands gallery. More than anything, Luis wanted local artists to prosper. Now that dream had become Cat's dream, too.

Cat could smell the coffee so she returned to the kitchen. She started breakfast – a typical and very simple Mexican breakfast. She cooked eggs and fried potatoes and wondered if her guest liked Mexican food. She found some *salsa verde* in an unopened glass jar on the shelf, and a chunk of cheese in the fridge. In the freezer, she found some frozen tortillas, thawed them out, and began frying them on the griddle. Not the best tortillas in the world, but better than no tortillas at all. She was just glad that she'd stopped off at the market for the eggs, potatoes, and coffee the night before. Going grocery shopping was on the list for today. She could hear Miles coming down the stairs. He appeared carrying a small backpack.

"Good morning," Cat said with a brief smile. "As I mentioned last night, I don't have any of that dark breakfast tea that you English dudes like to drink. I only have coffee."

"No problem. I like coffee, too."

In the light of day, Cat thought Miles looked different than he had last night. He was rested, or at least more than he had been. He seemed quite relaxed, like a man on vacation. He was dressed in jeans, a blue flannel shirt over a blue t-shirt, and hiking boots. His strawberry blond hair was tousled, and the stubble on his face was gone. His blue eyes were shining, and he was smiling. Cat couldn't help but notice that Miles Trevelyan was an attractive man. She gestured for him to sit down.

"The food isn't great, but it's better than nothing. I'm going shopping today."

He scooped both the eggs and fried potatoes onto a tortilla, then smeared the *salsa verde* on everything. "What's this?" he pointed to the cheese.

"That's *quesillo*. It's Oaxacan cheese."

Miles cut off a bite and tasted it. "Ummm….that's good." He turned up the lower end of his full tortilla to prevent anything from falling out of the bottom then neatly rolled it up. Half of the breakfast burrito went directly into his mouth.

"Where did you learn how to properly roll up a tortilla?"

He swallowed the first mouthful. "In Texas. McAllen to be exact. My first stop on my tour. First task. Learn how to make a proper burrito."

Cat watched him eat. He was an enthusiastic eater. He was rolling a second tortilla now, and he had cut off more of the *quesillo*. She was still working on her first burrito when he finished his second.

"This is so good." He smiled. "Thank you for breakfast."

Cat nodded. "I was wondering if you could tell me more about yourself and how it is that you came to rent a room from my brother. You know, we shared everything about our business plans. He never mentioned a bed and breakfast."

"I could be wrong about the B&B. It's possible that he was just renting the room out as a one-time deal. The B&B notion came from one of the people who directed me to Luis. She told me that a lot of people in Bisbee have opened B&Bs and rent out rooms during your busy season here. Maybe I just jumped to the conclusion that Luis was thinking of that. I don't really know for sure. After I wired the money to his attorney, Luis gave me a key to the back door and told me to text him a day or two before I was to arrive. I followed his instructions although I never got an answer to my text.

"What's this about wiring money to his lawyer?"

"Yes, I paid in advance. The lawyer's name is…," he hesitated. "It's Jeremy something. I forget his last name. It's a Spanish family name."

"Jeremy Flores?"

"That's right. Jeremy Flores. He didn't tell you?"

"I just came home to Bisbee. I haven't had a chance to see Jeremy. But I'll go see him this morning and find out about this. And there may be other things I need to know about, too." Cat frowned. "How much did Luis charge you?"

"About three hundred and eighty-five British pounds," Miles smiled. "Five hundred U.S. dollars."

"Wow. That's a good deal. Two weeks for five hundred dollars. Why did he give you such a good deal?"

"I think your brother liked me. He wanted to talk about the history of the Borderlands. He liked it that I am a scholar."

Cat nodded. "That sounds just like my brother. He liked to read, and he loved history. I think maybe Luis gave you a good deal in exchange for good conversation."

"The good deal also includes breakfast."

"*What*? Breakfast, too?" Cat snorted. "I'm not much of a cook. Are you ready for a bowl of cereal or eggs and tortillas every morning while you're here?"

"No problem. I like to cook. I'll make breakfast for us, m'lady."

"Why do you say that 'm'lady' thing?"

Miles shrugged his shoulders. "I'm an Englishman. And you seem like a lady to me." He reached for a third tortilla.

Cat couldn't help herself. She was surprised and unaccountably pleased to hear him say this.

"So you're working on a book? What's the book about?"

"About four hundred pages." He smiled.

Cat rolled her eyes. "You're such a smart ass." She couldn't help but smile a little.

"I'm a witty Englishman, not an American smart ass."

"Want to try again? What's your book about?" she repeated.

"My book will be about the U.S.-Mexico Borderlands. I started out studying the history of Mexico, specifically the post-1910 Revolutionary period. That was the subject of my dissertation and my first book. That led me to learn about a lot of interesting events on both sides of the border. From there, I became more and more interested in the entire U.S.-Mexico Borderlands, its history, culture, and the people who live here. I have found that the Borderlands are unique — not really American, not really Mexican."

"That's true."

He stared at his empty plate. "I probably ate too much. I like Mexican food. In my opinion, the food here is better than in Texas. Tucson has some really good restaurants."

"Yes, Sonoran cuisine is better than Tex-Mex. Everyone knows that except the Texans. Want more coffee?"

"Yes, please. Then I'd like to ask you some questions. We need to figure out why someone wants to get into your gallery and your living quarters."

"Like Englishmen who get really fabulous deals on a room and breakfast for a couple of weeks?"

"That's your good bloke. What about the bad bloke dressed all in black who broke in upstairs last night? Any ideas about who he was and what he wanted?"

"No," Cat frowned. "I have no idea. We've never had a break-in here."

"He may have thought that no one was here."

"Possibly. I just returned yesterday. My car is at the truck rental place. He probably saw the moving van outside but figured it was just parked there overnight."

"Do you think he wanted to steal some art?"

Cat shrugged her shoulders. "If that's the case, why not break in downstairs? He could have come in the back door. I doubt if it's that hard to break open. The kitchen windows also would be easy to get into, I think."

"Let's look in your gallery. Perhaps you can show me what's there."

They both rose and went into the main gallery. Paintings were on all four walls and there were a couple of sculptures on pedestals. A glass case against the back wall held some unique, original jewelry pieces that looked more like sculpture than jewelry.

Miles stopped in front of a painting that dominated one wall. At eight feet tall and five feet wide, the painting dwarfed all other paintings in the gallery. It had diagonal stripes in shades of gray across the canvas with three huge pairs of human lips in black topped by three additional images of lips in red and orange, ready to give someone a kiss. Miles looked closer at the placard attached to the wall. It read: "Kissed." Then the artist's name. Jax Beringer.

"The title is 'Kissed'?"

"That's right."

"What does it mean? Why is it so big?"

"I don't know," Cat said. "Luis hung it not long before I came back here to take care of him. Luis said he put it up for gallery visitors to see the latest Jax Beringer painting. Beringer is an up-and-coming artist. Luis sold a lot of his paintings, mainly online through our website."

"So Jax Beringer lives in Bisbee?"

"Yes. I only met him once and just briefly. I thought he was kind of a *pendejo*. Oh, do you know that word? You speak Spanish?"

"Yes, I speak a little. That word means 'arsehole,' right?"

Cat nodded. "Luis introduced us one weekend when I came home for a visit. Honestly, within five minutes of meeting me, he was hitting on me and making sexually suggestive comments." She wrinkled up her nose. "He was really arrogant. He seemed to think he was God's gift to women."

"So Luis represented Beringer mainly for financial purposes? Not because they were friends?"

"That's correct. I don't think Beringer was such a dick at first, but he got more demanding all the time."

"Do you have more of his paintings? Are they the most valuable of all the artists you represent?"

"Yes and yes. His paintings have greater financial value than any of our other artists. There are a couple of smaller ones on that wall." She gestured behind her. "And we have at least ten in storage. Maybe more. I have to do an inventory. That's a key issue. We have in our possession a bunch of his paintings and a firm, legal contract to sell them. Jax Beringer moved to Bisbee a couple of years ago from Los Angeles. I never understood why he came here. Not long after he arrived, Luis signed a contract to represent Beringer. Luis was the one who really helped Beringer get established. Beringer's career took off when Luis started representing him. But Beringer felt no loyalty or gratitude toward Luis at all. Beringer now wants to break the contract and start selling his paintings himself. Or sell through an upscale New York City gallery. I'm not sure what his plan is. We figured he would leave here and go on to New York City. Apparently he thinks he can become famous in New York and make a lot of money."

"Any chance Beringer might be the one who broke in last night?

"Unlikely. Beringer disappeared a month before I came back here to take care of Luis. So he's been gone like three or four months." Cat frowned.

"Interesting. Did the police look into this?"

"Yes, the Cochise County Sheriff did an investigation. There was no sign of foul play. And absolutely no sign of Jax Beringer. He seemed to have walked out of his house without even looking back."

"Do you think he might have been abducted or something?"

"Maybe. Who knows? Do you want to know what *I* think happened?"

"Yes, of course."

"I think it's some kind of publicity stunt. I think Jax Beringer figures if he disappears for a while, he'll become this mysterious, sexy, enigmatic artist. I think he thinks it will make his work more desirable to collectors. I bet he's on a beach somewhere drinking margaritas and plotting his triumphant return to the art world."

"So back to square one. Is there anything upstairs that a thief might consider valuable?"

"Not that I know of. Luis had a laptop, which is in his closet. I brought in stuff like my computer and a little television. I have a little bit of jewelry but nothing very valuable. He had all those books."

"Yes, I noticed that bookshelves completely cover one wall in his room. He has…had a very good collection, especially history books. But I doubt a thief would be interested in that unless Luis had a rare first edition or something."

"I don't think he had anything valuable like that."

"Let's go back to your kitchen. I could use another cup of coffee."

They returned to the kitchen, and Cat poured Miles another cup.

Cat began cutting up a cantaloupe. She placed the plate full of pieces on the table and handed Miles a fork. She took her fork and chose a piece.

"I don't want to make you uncomfortable, but is there any chance the intruder wasn't after some *thing* but instead, some *one*?"

"What do you mean?" Cat asked.

"A woman all alone in the house?"

"Oh god. Am I going to have to start worrying about *that*?"

"We have to consider everything."

They fell silent and sipped their coffee.

"I'm glad you were here last night," Cat said finally. She smiled.

"Me, too."

"I'm so sorry about all this. You should be having fun."

"No need to apologize. I actually find this very intriguing. I can work on the book anytime. But to find myself in the middle of a mystery, fighting off banditos and drinking coffee with such a charming and lovely señorita is infinitely more interesting than organizing my notes. Luis was right. You are very sweet."

At that, the smile disappeared from Cat's face. Tears filled her eyes and began rolling down her cheeks. She clasped her hands in her lap and suppressed a sob.

"Oh god," Miles blurted at the sight of her tears. "I'm such an idiot. A total clod. I didn't mean to hurt you. Please forgive me."

Cat looked up. Miles had a genuinely distressed look on his face. She managed a small smile.

"It's okay. I'm still kind of raw. I miss my brother. I know you meant well. You are very kind." She found a paper napkin and wiped her eyes. "So what are you going to do today, Mr. Bloke?" She smiled and tried to lighten the mood.

Miles returned her smile. "This morning I plan to just go for a little walk around Bisbee and reacquaint myself. Unless you think I should stay here with you."

"Nah. I'll be okay. Do you know about the trail that goes along the mountainside above the town?

"No. Tell me. I quite enjoy hiking. That will go first on the list of things to do."

"The trailhead is close to here. I'll show you when you get ready to leave."

"And you. What will you do today?"

"I'm going to go see my lawyer, Jeremy Flores. I'd like to find out if there will be any more surprises in addition to an Englishman showing up in the middle of the night. I guess I should call the local police and report the intruder, too. Then this afternoon, I'll continue unloading the moving van and haul everything upstairs."

"Oh, you'll have to let me to help you with that."

"No. You should be having fun here, not doing manual labor."

"It'll be my pleasure. It's just too bad that you don't have a lift."

"A lift?" Cat looked puzzled. "Oh, yeah, a lift. Hey, you want to hear a dumb joke?"

"Certainly."

"Okay, so there were these two dudes. One American and one British."

"You mean a dude and a bloke."

Cat rolled her eyes. "Whatever. So the English bloke was in the elevator…"

"The lift?"

"Miles, be quiet and listen."

"Okay. I'm listening." He chuckled.

"The American dude came running up and said, 'Wait! Wait!' The English bloke pressed the stop button, and the American got into the elevator. He turned to the Englishman and said, 'Thanks so much for holding the elevator for me.'"

"'You mean 'lift' said the Englishman.' 'No, I mean 'elevator,'' said the American."

Miles was grinning now.

"The Englishman said, 'We English invented the language, you know.'"

Cat paused, smiling. "The American said, 'Well, we Americans invented the elevator.'"

Miles laughed. "Touché."

Cat smiled. "Pretty dumb joke, huh?"

"It's nice to see your smile." Miles stood up and took his cup to the sink. "If you will be so kind to show me the trailhead, I'll be off on my morning trek."

"Sure. Come with me."

They went back through the gallery and Cat unlocked the front door. She pointed up the hill. "See those madrone trees?"

"The ones with the red trunks and branches?"

"That's right. That's where the trail is. So you go up the street. See that big rock? There's a short trail behind the rock that goes up to the main trail where the madrone trees are. The trail is well-marked and easy to follow. It will take you all the way along Tombstone Canyon. You'll end up above the main Bisbee business district. All along the way, you'll see smaller trails and paved walkways with lots of stairs that take you down into town."

"Great." He shifted his backpack onto his back. Miles hesitated. "I have a favor to ask of you, m'lady."

"And what would that be, *guapo*?"

He smiled. "Will you please keep your doors locked when you're here as well as when you're gone? Please."

"Of course. After that intruder last night, I don't want to make things easy for him."

Miles hesitated. "Okay, then. I'm going. See you later." He took off at a stride toward the trail. Once on the trail, he looked back and waved.

Cat waved and went back inside.

She stopped in her tracks. Oh no! She had called Miles *guapo*. She wondered how well he understood Spanish. Did he know that she called him 'handsome?' She didn't want him to get the wrong idea. Get a grip, Cat. Okay, so he's good looking. Yes, very attractive and charming, too. But he's only here for a short time, and the last thing she needed right now was to get involved with a man. She wanted to learn more about Luis's plans, and most of all, she had to find out why someone tried to break into her house.

* * *

Miles had done his best to appear confident and relaxed so as to not further distress the lovely Señorita Miranda. Obviously, she was distracted by her grief and not in the most alert frame of mind to be watching out for anyone who might pose a danger to her. He would do his best to step in and watch out for her. Perhaps before his time in Bisbee was over, they would be able to resolve any vulnerabilities she might have going forward. He wanted her to be safe.

He easily found the long trail and within minutes, he was meandering along through the madrone trees and cacti of various species, enjoying the intense blue sky, the red hills and the lovely little town below.

Miles smiled to himself. Cat had called him '*guapo*' when she answered him. He knew that *guapo* meant 'handsome' in Spanish. He would like very much for the lovely Miss Miranda to find him attractive as well as kind. As for himself, he decided that she was the loveliest woman he'd met in a long time, maybe ever. She was a Borderlands woman.

He whistled as he walked.

3 Visitors

Cat did as Miles requested. She went around the ground floor and made sure all doors and windows were locked. Then she did the same upstairs. She hesitated to go into the room occupied by Miles. He should have his privacy. Also, the room still belonged to Luis in her mind, and she couldn't stop the sad memories of sitting with him as he wasted away. She knew it would take a while before the sadness eased. She hoped she would be able to focus on all the good times she'd had with her big brother.

She looked into the room and saw that Miles had secured the door to the deck. Anyone attempting to enter there would have to break the glass.

A quick phone call to attorney Jeremy Flores came next. Jeremy apologized three or four times in their brief conversation, but he made it clear that he couldn't spend more than a few minutes with her.

Cat decided to walk to Jeremy's office, which was located in downtown Bisbee. The word "downtown" always made her smile because the word made it sound like Bisbee was much bigger than it really was. In fact, fewer than six thousand people lived in the spread-out city of Bisbee. Old Bisbee, the downtown area, was where all the tourists visited. The best restaurants and bars, shops, and music venues were found in the narrow, steep-walled Tombstone Canyon with all its colorful houses and many staircases that led to houses and streets on the upper hillsides. Old Bisbee was the heart of a small town that also included several satellite communities. The thought occurred to Cat then that later she would take Miles Trevelyan on a driving tour of the communities of Warren, Lowell, and San Jose and some smaller neighborhoods that were included in the "city of Bisbee." She thought he'd be interested in learning about her hometown. Miles seemed interested in everything about her part of the world.

The central road through Tombstone Canyon tilted downward slightly, and she made good time. She arrived at Jeremy Flores's office in only ten minutes. She opened the door and walked in. There was no one at the receptionist's desk.

"Hey, Jeremy. Are you here?" she called out.

"Yeah, I'm here. Come on back."

Cat and Jeremy had gone to high school together. He went off to university and law school. She went to university and to work in Phoenix. He had come home to Bisbee last year, and now it was her turn. She remembered him from high school as being smart and cocky, a prankster and teller of jokes. He was a small man, never very involved in athletics, more dependent on his brains than brawn. Once when they were both home on university holiday, she and Jeremy had gone across the border to Naco to hear a *cumbia* band and to drink beer. She learned from their conversation that he was also an idealist who saw the law as a way to help people. She liked him, and she admired him, too.

Cat walked into Jeremy's office. It was a mess. Stacks of papers on his desk, on the floor, on the chairs in front of his desk, everywhere. Jeremy was a mess, too. His dress shirt was rumpled, his necktie lose around his neck. He looked exhausted.

"Jeez, Jeremy. What's going on with you? Where's your office receptionist? Are you getting any sleep?"

"The receptionist won't be here for another hour. No, I'm not getting much sleep, Cat. You know when I signed on to work at this firm, I had a senior partner, Abe Meyer. He and I were going to work together, and he was going to mentor me."

"I heard that he died suddenly."

"Yeah, Abe had a heart attack about a week after I arrived. I'm on my own now. I have too much work, plus I'm dealing with a lot of new stuff that I'm not all that familiar with. I haven't been out of law school that long." He paused, "Don't tell anyone I said that. I don't want anyone to lose confidence in me."

"I won't. And for the record, I have complete confidence in you."

"Your stuff is actually pretty easy," Jeremy said. "Luis left a will, and all his papers are in order. You and Luis are formal business partners with inheritance rights if the other partner dies. And he left all his personal possessions to you, too. We'll just have to go through the probate process, but I see no problem at all."

"So what's keeping you so busy?"

"First, I volunteered to help out some of the Central American migrants at the border who are attempting to get asylum. That's a huge job. I could work there full time. But I'm a volunteer and get no pay so I can't very well do that. And I have my regular work here. On top of that, this investor group of outsiders has purchased a big acreage in Bisbee's San Jose district. The outsiders want to put in a housing development. I'm representing a group of citizens concerned about water resources, environmental damage, traffic, all the problems that come with development. There's a concern about how the San Pedro River will be affected if all these houses go in."

"Not to be all motherly, but if you get so worn out that you get sick, you won't be able to do anything at all. You have to take care of yourself."

"My wife is upset with me, too. She says she never sees me. She's worried about my health, too."

Cat nodded sympathetically.

"Yes, you're right," Jeremy added. "I just don't know how to prioritize. I'm not taking on any more clients, and I'm going to cut back on some of this stuff. I need some rest." He looked at Cat directly. "You're just as pretty as you always were."

"Oh, stop it. I'm just a typical Mexican girl. Thanks, though."

"A very pretty typical Mexican girl."

"I won't tell your wife you said that," she smiled.

"Not to worry. My wife is the most beautiful girl in the world, and I'm crazy about her. What can I do for you anyway?"

"This British dude showed up at my house late last night. He said Luis rented him a room for a couple of weeks. I want to make sure he's legit, and also to ask you if there are any other surprises Luis left for me."

Jeremy turned and opened a door on one of three filing cabinets. He pulled out a file folder and began shuffling papers.

"Miles Trevelyan? Is that your man?"

"Yes. He claims he paid in advance for a room and breakfast."

Jeremy looked at her and nodded. "Yes, he paid in advance. Wired the money to Luis's account." He grinned. "And who is going to make breakfast for this Englishman?"

"Me, I guess." She shook her head and chuckled. "Poor dude. Stuck with a bowl of cold cereal every morning. Or burritos. He seems to like burritos. Anything else I should know?"

"About him, I don't think so. Well, you know about the acreage that Luis bought over in San Jose a couple of years ago. Other than that, I see your tenants have given notice that they are moving in a couple of months."

"*What*? Acres of land? Tenants? What are you talking about?" Cat was genuinely surprised.

"Luis bought that house next door to the gallery a few months ago. It's yours now because he left it to you. There's an older couple living there. They've decided to move back to Tucson to be nearer their kids and grandkids. The twenty acres are just west of San Jose. It's undeveloped. Just open desert."

"I don't know what to say. I didn't know about any of this. The house right next door? I guess I better go over and introduce myself. Anything else I need to know?"

"No, but we may have an ongoing problem with that artist Luis represents, Jax Beringer. He wanted to contest his contract with your gallery and get it nullified when he disappeared. He'll be a problem when he shows up again."

"I bet he'll be a problem. He's just a pain in the butt. Any other surprises?"

"I don't think so. Luis was a very organized person. When we worked on his will, he talked about how much he loved you and how grateful he was for you taking care of him in his final days. My bet is that he bought the house as a nice surprise for you."

Cat felt her eyes filling with tears again. She stood up.

"Thanks, Jeremy. I won't take any more of your time. I appreciate all you did for Luis and all you're doing for me. Let me know when you need me to come by again. I guess I better go buy some groceries so I can feed this Brit. It's a good thing he likes Mexican food."

She headed toward the door then turned back. "Also I want to mention that someone tried to break into my house last night. He came up the back stairs into Luis's room, but Trevelyan was there and chased him off."

Jeremy frowned. "You'd better call Sam Morales and report this."

"That's next on my list. Thanks, Jeremy. I hope things get easier for you."

* * *

Cat retrieved her car and drove to the big Safeway in Bisbee's San Jose district. She bought a lot of fresh fruit and veggies, fresh tortillas, chicken, eggs, and other items that she thought she could manage. She wasn't a bad cook. She just had never given it all that much attention. But she obviously had to fulfill her obligation to provide Mr. Miles Trevelyan something decent to eat every morning. Something Mexican. He seemed to be very enthusiastic about Mexican food. On her way home, she purchased some fresh tamales from a woman selling them out of her car in the parking lot.

When she arrived home, Cat put the groceries away. Just as she finished, Cat heard a light knocking sound on the front glass door of the gallery. She went into the gallery and saw a man standing there peering into the gallery.

Cat went to the front door, unlocked it, and opened the door.

"I'm sorry, but we're not open now. We won't be opening our doors probably for another week or two."

"Oh, too bad. I came all the way from Los Angeles. I wanted to take a look at works by Jax Beringer."

Cat frowned. She didn't want to deal with gallery visitors right now with so much going on. At the same time, she also didn't want to turn away a potential client, especially one who had come from so far. She and Luis had discussed how important it was to develop a national clientele to support the gallery and local artists. And they still had several Beringer paintings to sell.

She made an effort to smile, stepped back and opened the door wider. "Well, okay, come on in. But don't tell anyone I let you in. I'm still unpacking and getting ready for a big opening next month."

As the man passed her, she noticed he was rather nondescript looking. He was fairly tall, though not as tall as Miles, slightly overweight and dressed in casual clothes. He looked like the typical tourist. He wouldn't be noticed in a crowd.

"Thank you so much. My name is Freddy Hubbard. I teach at a community college in Glendale. I'm a fan of Jax Beringer's art."

"Take a look around. There's that big one titled 'Kissed' and two smaller ones on the opposite wall."

"These are all you have?"

"No, we have more, but we won't take those out of storage until we get ready for the opening next month."

Hubbard was standing in front of "Kissed."

"Do you know what this painting is all about? Most of his work is very abstract. This one is less so. And what about those big lips?"

Cat noticed that his demeanor had changed. He had a frown on his face now.

"Sorry. I can't tell you. My brother took this in and hung it. But my brother passed away recently. I don't know much about this painting. I just moved here from Phoenix."

"So you're new here? I've been thinking about investing in a gallery in this part of the world. Have you considered selling this gallery?"

He was smiling, but to Cat, he seemed different now. Serious. Even a bit nervous.

Cat shook her head. "No, I'm here for the long term. I have plans for our gallery."

Hubbard nodded. "Also, I heard you have a David Hockney watercolor you might be willing to sell."

Cat frowned in confusion. She shook her head. "No, Hockney is very famous. A work of his, even a watercolor, would be worth a lot of money. We're not at that level. We don't handle anything that expensive. Anyway, Hockney is British. We only represent regional artists."

Hubbard nodded.

Cat picked up a brochure about the gallery from a small table near the front door. "Take this. You can stay in touch with us online. Perhaps you'll become interested in some of our artists from southern Arizona and northern Sonora."

"Northern Sonora?"

"That's the Mexican state just south of our border. I mean south of the state of Arizona. Sonora is also the name of this desert we live in."

"I see. Okay. Well, thanks for letting me look at the artwork."

Cat opened the door for Hubbard. She watched him walk away downhill toward the main road through Tombstone Canyon. How odd, she thought. He barely glanced at the art except for the "Kissed" painting. What made him think she might sell the gallery? And why on earth would he think that she and Luis had artwork by David Hockney?

She stood there absent-mindedly staring at the display case at the back wall of the gallery while she punched in the number for the Bisbee police department.

Sam Morales, Bisbee's police chief, answered.

"Hey, Sam. This is Cat Miranda."

"Hi Cat. I heard you were coming home. Glad to have you back in Bisbee."

"How's your wife and kids?"

"Just fine. The kids are a handful. I let Julia deal with them. She threatens to starve them if they don't act civilized." He laughed. "Are you getting settled in?"

"Sort of. I returned yesterday. I'm still unpacking. I'm calling because there was an intruder last night who broke into my place. I have a guest staying here, Miles Trevelyan. He's a visiting scholar from the U.K. Luis rented him a room before he got so sick. Trevelyan is the one who chased off the intruder."

She gave the police chief details of the intruder coming up the back stairs and encountering Miles Trevelyan in Luis's room.

"I'll come by later and take a look. Then I'll write a report up about this in case it happens again. It's good to hear there was a man there to stop this intruder."

"Thanks, Sam. I don't think there's much more that you can do right now. See you later."

They said their goodbyes just as Cat heard another knock on the front glass.

This time there were two people at the door, a man and a woman.

Guess this is going to be one of those days, Cat said to herself.

She went to the door, opened it and said, "I'm sorry, but we're not open now. We'll be having a big opening next month."

The woman spoke first. "Actually we came to see you, Miss Miranda."

She and the man pushed past Cat and stood just inside the gallery door.

"My name is Helen Fuller, and this is my husband, Nolan Fuller." She stuck out her hand.

Cat shook hands with her and also with her husband.

"We live here in Bisbee."

"Oh, nice to meet you," Cat said. She had never seen these two before. She judged them to be maybe in their forties or early fifties, well-dressed, and with an air of confidence around them that Cat associated with affluence.

Helen spoke in a friendly way, but Cat could tell she wanted something. Nolan Fuller also had a polite smile on his face. At the same time, he gazed openly at Cat as if he were evaluating her. He, too, wanted something.

"What can I do for you?" Cat asked.

"We moved here from southern California a couple of years ago. We know you only recently returned to Bisbee. We also know your brother died recently. Sorry for your loss."

Cat was trying not to get irritated. How do they know all this? And those were just empty words about Luis. What did they really want?

"We're interested in opening an art gallery. We're here to ask you to consider selling this gallery to us. We would make you a very good offer," Helen Fuller said.

So that's it. They want the gallery. No way, Cat thought.

"I haven't even thought about selling, and Luis and I….."

Before Cat could finish, Nolan Fuller spoke. He was still smiling. His voice had an unusual reedy quality, but it was firm, like a man accustomed to giving orders and having them followed without question.

"We know that Luis Miranda was the main force behind this gallery. Your role was to help with graphic design. When he died, you were forced to return to Bisbee and leave behind a good job in Phoenix."

Cat frowned. Fuller seemed to know a lot about her personal life.

Helen spoke up. Her approach wasn't quite as blunt. "We were just thinking that your life has been disrupted. Perhaps you'd like to be rid of this huge responsibility, a burden even, and return to your life in Phoenix."

"I think you may have misunderstood my relationship with my brother," Cat said. "We were business partners. I had a greater role than simply doing graphic design for the gallery." She paused and realized that she didn't want to reveal much more about herself and what she and Luis had planned for the gallery.

"But you left so much behind in Phoenix," Helen said. She spoke to Cat as if Cat were a three-year old and needed coaxing to eat her vegetables.

"Not really. I'm happy to be home. I grew up in Bisbee, you know." She stepped back and opened the door again. "I'm very sorry, but this gallery is not for sale."

Nolan Fuller smiled, but the smile did not reach his eyes. "You think about it. I believe you'll change your mind. We will make it worth your while."

"Thanks for coming by. I hope to see you at the opening next month," Cat said politely. Both Fullers hesitated then moved through the front door to the outside. Cat closed the door behind her, locked it, and walked to the back of the gallery.

Damn. Maybe if they attend the opening, they'll see that she was serious about running the gallery. She hoped she wouldn't see them again until next month. Getting two offers to sell in the same day was totally unexpected. Weird really.

Cat headed for the kitchen to make another cup of coffee. Before she got there, she turned back to make sure there was no one else at the front door. That's when she noticed an odd glint on the polished wooden floor in front of the painting "Kissed." She approached, bent down and touched the floor. Her hand came up wet.

"Oh, no!" Cat groaned. A leak! There was water leaking slowly from under the painting. She must have a serious plumbing problem. She needed to get the leak stopped before it ruined any art or the polished wooden floor. She ran for her phone and called the only plumber she knew, her former high school classmate Eric Carter. She explained the problem and her urgency.

"I'll be right there, Cat. I just finished a job so I'm free for the rest of the day."

Ten minutes later, Eric Carter showed up in his van which had "Carter's Plumbing" in big blue letters on the side. Cat was mopping up the leak with towels when she heard him knock at the back door.

"Cat, I'll go turn the water off at the main street valve. Back in a minute."

When he returned, Eric said, "Cat, I'll find the leak, fix it and have your water back on pretty quickly. But first, we're going to have to move that big painting. I think the leak is in the wall behind it."

Cat nodded. She left the gallery and returned with a small ladder. Together they unfastened the painting "Kissed" from the wall and moved it to the back of the gallery next to the jewelry display case.

"Yep, see where water has been seeping through the wall? I'm going to have to tear out part of the wall to get to the pipe. Then I'll replace the dry wall. You can go to the hardware store and get some paint and paint it yourself. Save your money that way. I think I can be finished in a couple of hours."

"That's great," Cat said. "I'll get out of your way." She headed for the kitchen.

Seconds later, Miles entered the back door with several grocery bags in hand. He had used his key. "Hello, m'lady. I went shopping."

"I see that. We're going to have plenty of food."

"As I said, cooking is becoming a kind of hobby for me. That is, if you will be so kind as to allow me to use your kitchen?"

"No problem. *Mi casa es tu casa.*"

"I understand that phrase. You're saying your house is my house."

"That's right."

"I'll put this away, and then I'll help you carry your things upstairs."

"It's a deal," Cat paused. "Also you should know we have no running water right now. We have a leak in the gallery wall, and the plumber is working on it now. He says it won't take long."

Miles did as promised. He put away his groceries and followed Cat out to the moving van. He chose the heaviest boxes, and within fifteen minutes, all of Cat's possessions were upstairs, either in her room or on the landing.

"Thank you so much, m'lord. Should I call you m'lord?"

"Not really necessary. I'm low on the totem pole. That's what you say? Totem pole?"

"Yes. What do you mean, low on the totem pole? Oh my god, are you really a lord?"

Miles laughed. "Just a baronet."

"What's a baronet?"

"A bloke with a clarinet. You know? Baronet. Clarinet."

"Oh." Cat looked confused. "Why not clarinetist?"

Miles laughed. "I'm teasing you."

She shook her head and sighed. "Okay, smart ass. So tell me. What's a baronet?"

"A baronet is a hereditary title, the lowest title awarded by the British Crown. One of my ancestors was responsible for the title. No need for you to be impressed."

Cat's eyes were wide. "So I'm supposed to call you Lord Miles?"

"No. 'Sir' will be acceptable." He chuckled.

Cat giggled. "Okay, Sir Miles."

"Or you can just call me *guapo*." Miles grinned.

Oh gosh. Cat slapped her forehead with her hand.

That made Miles laugh out loud.

"You speak Spanish, don't you?"

"*Te lo dije. Hablo un poco.* I told you. I speak a little. Come on, m'lady. Let's make something hot to drink. We can use bottled water until the plumber gets everything fixed."

Cat followed Miles into her kitchen.

4 In the Wall

While they made coffee, Miles and Cat could hear Eric using an electric saw to cut away portions of the wall.

"Here it is," he called out. "There's a corroded pipe with a big hole in it. It will be easy to replace." He paused. "What the hell is this?"

Cat heard nothing but silence for a couple of minutes.

"Cat, you better come and look at this." Eric Carter's voice was different now. Serious.

Oh rats, she said to herself. He's going to tell her that her entire *pinche* building needs to be re-plumbed.

Cat and Miles went into the gallery.

"Eric Carter, meet Miles Trevelyan. Miles is here for a couple of weeks." Cat gestured to them both.

Eric didn't respond or even look at Miles. He was staring at a big opening in the gallery wall. At his eye level and slightly to the left, Cat could see an old metal pipe with obvious corrosion. A few drops of water were still leaking from the big, ragged hole in the pipe. She looked at Eric. He was looking into the opening in the wall. His gaze went to his right a few feet from the pipe and down near the floor. Cat's eyes followed his.

"*Oh my god!*" Cat cried out as she jumped back in horror. "There's a body. There's a dead body in there. *Oh no!*"

Miles moved closer. He frowned.

Eric turned to Cat. His face was pale. "You'd better call Sam Morales. Maybe call the sheriff's department, too. Someone stuffed a dead body in your wall."

Cat turned and retrieved her phone. Her hands were shaking, but somehow she managed to call the Bisbee city police department again and report what Eric Carter had found in her wall. Then she called the Cochise County Sheriff's office. In both cases, she was told that all deputies were out on calls. It would be an hour or more before anyone could be there.

Cat told Miles and Eric that it would be a while before law enforcement arrived. Then she stood there staring at the gallery floor, her arms wrapped around her. She was trembling.

"Eric, Cat, let's go and sit on the back porch," Miles said.

They followed him out and sat at the table there under the *portál*. Miles disappeared for a few minutes and returned with two bottles of Tres Equis beer and a small glass of red wine. Eric nodded gratefully and opened his bottle. He drained it immediately.

"Here, Cat, take a sip of this." Miles handed her the wine glass.

She looked at Miles with tears in her eyes.

"Please," he said. "Just a sip." She complied as he opened his own bottle. Miles drank half the bottle.

"Here's what I saw," Miles said. "I saw the body of a deceased man slumped up against the back wall. He wasn't big or heavy, but then, it was obvious that his body had undergone some significant desiccation in this arid desert environment. The man's skin was a light brown, shriveled and leather-like. His eyes were closed, and his mouth partially open. Teeth were visible. His entire face was sunken with bones protruding under the withered and wrinkled skin."

Miles glanced at his companions. Eric was listening and nodding. Cat was still hugging herself and trembling. She was pale.

"Take another sip, Cat," Miles said. "This is difficult, but if we relax, focus, and bring our intellect and observations to this, we'll make a better report to law enforcement. I'm drawing on what I learned in a class I took once in the history of forensics."

Cat looked at him and nodded. "I'll try, Miles."

Miles continued, "The man was dressed in jeans and a long-sleeved, patterned cotton shirt. There were dark red stains both on the shirt and pants. Those are probably blood stains. His hair also appeared to be clumped together in strands that had been wet, then dried. Probably blood caused the clumping. His hands and feet were also uncovered, no shoes."

"He had a small circular gold earring in one ear and no rings on his hands," Cat added.

"He had some kind of tattoo on what I could see of his chest," Eric said.

"I also noticed numerous small circular indentations on the skin that were easily visible. On his face primarily," Miles said.

"Yes, I noticed that, too," Eric said. "The circular indentations are about the size of the head of a hammer or a similar tool."

"And there was a kind of little notch in the circle," Cat added.

Eric nodded.

"We may be looking at the effects of the murder weapon," Miles said.

They fell silent.

Then Miles asked, "Do either of you know who this man is?"

Eric Carter shook his head no.

Cat looked down at her hands, then at Miles, "Oh god. I think I do know him. I think we're looking at the body of Jax Beringer, that artist who disappeared a couple of months ago. I thought he just ran off but now…." Her voice trailed away.

"Very good, Cat. Very observant," Miles said.

More silence.

Eric spoke first. "Look. The only thing I know about forensics is what I see on TV. You know? All those cop shows? Usually they don't like anyone messing with a crime scene."

"Crime scene?" Cat groaned.

"Yeah," Eric continued. "But I think I'm going to go in there and fix that pipe. The hole is several feet to the left of the body. I can fix it without disturbing anything. Then I can get your water back on. If I don't do that, the cops will set up a crime scene, and you won't be able to live in this house with no water until they take down their yellow tape. Or am I living in a television cop-show reality too much?"

"No," Miles said. "I think you're right. They will no doubt be concerned about preserving the crime scene."

Eric slapped his palms on his thighs. "That's what I'm going to do. I'm going to fix that leak." He went back into gallery, and within a few minutes, they could hear the sounds of his tools.

"Let's sit on the swing," Miles said.

Cat followed him and sat down next to him in the wooden swing near the back door. They sat together in silence.

"You're so calm," she said.

Miles smiled. "It's my British reserve. Stiff upper lip and all that. You, on the other hand, are a delightful mix of Mexican and American expressiveness. You're expressing your distress now."

"'Distress' is such a nice word for what I feel. It sounds way better than 'semi-hysterical.' You make being distressed sound almost normal."

"What you are feeling is completely appropriate. You've had a lot to deal with lately."

More silence.

"May I hold your hand?" Miles asked quietly.

Cat smiled. "You're so polite."

"I told you last night that I would be on my best behavior. I don't want to distress you even more by being too bold."

Cat reached out and took his hand. "I think holding your hand will be a comfort to me."

They sat together for a while saying nothing.

Finally Cat spoke. "Miles, I don't understand why you're still here. Most people on vacation would demand a return of their money and get the hell out of Bisbee as soon as possible when confronted with the intruder last night, and now this. Why are you still here?"

"Before I left England, I went to visit my dad for about a week."

"And your mom, too?"

"No, Mum passed away a couple of years ago."

"I'm sorry," she said. "I really mean that."

Miles nodded. "My dad and I sat down together, and we had a heart-to-heart talk. He told me that he would worry about me because traveling along the U.S.-Mexico border meant going into a conflict zone. He asked me to stay in touch often."

Cat frowned when she heard that. "Well, I guess he's right about that. What's your dad's name?"

"Ian Trevelyan. I promised to text and email him frequently so he'd know I was okay. Then he said something really interesting and wise, I think. He told me to treat every person I meet on this trip as my teacher. He said even the ones that made me angry or those I disagreed with would have a lesson for me."

"Yes, your dad does sound very wise."

"Cat, I'm staying here because this is quite an unusual situation for me. You are what's happening now. That makes you my teacher. I think there is something for me to learn from you."

"Gosh, I have no idea what that might be."

"We'll discover that as we go along, I think. There's a second reason, too."

"What's that?"

"I like you. Luis was quite correct. You are very sweet. I want you to be safe. I'm here to help you solve this mystery of intruders breaking in and dead bodies and whatever else comes up so that you will be safe."

Cat's eyes filled with tears.

"But I don't want to make you cry." Miles frowned.

Cat groaned. "I'm just expressing. Isn't that what you called it? Expressing? I like you, too. I accept your offer of help. God knows I need it. I just wish I could stop crying."

Eric Carter reappeared at the back door. "All fixed, Cat. You may have to think about re-plumbing at some point. But for now, you have no more leaks, and I turned the water back on."

"Okay, let me pay you."

"Let's not mess with that now. The police will be here soon. I'll send you an invoice."

Cat nodded. "Thanks, Eric."

At that moment, they heard footsteps approaching from the side of the house. Sam Morales, the Bisbee police chief, appeared.

"I heard you talking so I came back here."

"Sam, you know Eric. This is Miles Trevelyan. He's my guest."

"Cat told me about the intruder last night. I'm really glad you were here, Mr. Trevelyan," Morales said.

Miles nodded. "I'm afraid things are even more serious now. We have a dead body in the wall of Cat's gallery."

"I'll need a statement from each of you. Eric, let's start with you since you found the body. Show me."

The two men disappeared. Miles and Cat sat together holding hands.

Soon the policeman Sam Morales and the plumber Eric Carter reappeared.

"I'm off, Cat. I'll send you an invoice, and if you have any more plumbing problems, let me know." Eric Carter waved goodbye.

"Mr. Trevelyan, I need a statement from you." Sam Morales stepped forward.

"I don't have much to say. I arrived late last night. You know about the intruder who was here. I left this morning for a while, and I came back here about an hour ago. That's when the plumber alerted us to the body in the wall. I don't know who this man is. But it seems rather obvious that he's been dead a month or more. I'm sure your medical examiner will be able to pin that down. Your arid desert environment has led to significant desiccation of the corpse."

"Cat, Eric said you think you know who the dead man is."

"Yes, Jax Beringer."

"That's what I think, too," Morales agreed. "I met Beringer a couple of times before he disappeared. I think now we know why he disappeared."

"When exactly was that?" Miles asked.

"Two months back."

"So he could have been dead as long two months." Miles concluded.

"But he couldn't have been in the wall that long," Cat added.

"Why do you say that?" Morales asked.

"Luis was here during that time. He was really sick. Then he died a month ago. I was here, too, for most of that time, too. I was taking care of Luis."

"So that means that the only time someone could have put him in the wall was after Luis died and you had returned to Phoenix, Cat," Miles added. "That means Beringer was killed in another location, and his body put into your wall when you weren't here."

"I think you're right about that. I stayed here a week after Luis died. We had a memorial service for him. Then I returned to Phoenix for more than three weeks. I went to my job to clear up everything. I cleaned out my apartment and loaded everything into the moving van. I came home just two days ago."

Sam Morales was taking notes on everything Cat and Miles said. "Okay. So Beringer disappeared. And it looks like he was murdered."

"Yes, all three of us noticed a large number of circular indentations on the body. I'm speculating that he was beaten to death," Miles said.

Sam Morales nodded.

"Yes, those marks were on his face and neck and even on his hands. I think he was hit repeatedly with something really hard," Cat added. "Eric thought maybe a hammer."

"Anything else you noticed?" Sam Morales asked.

"It must be meaningful that the body was behind Beringer's painting," Cat added.

"Or that could just be because the painting was so big that it covered where the wall had been cut into to stash the body."

"Maybe," said Cat, "but I don't think so. I mean, if you're going to hide a body, the fact that it was hidden in an art gallery and behind the artist's work just has to mean something. The killer could have left the body anywhere but chose the gallery intentionally. It took effort to break in to the gallery, remove the painting, cut open the wall, put the body there, patch up the wall, and put the painting back where it was. And not be noticed by anyone."

"I agree," said Miles.

Sam Morales nodded. "Probably right about that. This is starting to have the feeling of revenge. Something really personal."

Miles added, "It appears possible that someone really hated Beringer. The murderer can gloat about the body's location even if it is never found. Kind of a nasty little secret. And if the body *is* found, having hidden it behind a huge painting done by the murdered artist is a way of dismissing and disrespecting the dead man's artwork and the man himself."

Cat nodded in agreement.

"Cat, I'll probably have some more questions later, but right now, I'm going to set up a crime scene with yellow tape. I'll take a bunch of photos of the scene, too. When I get back to my office, I'll send word that we need a crime scene investigation team to come in from Tucson. They most likely won't come until tomorrow. The next step will be for me to contact one of the local funeral homes to retrieve the body. The body will be transported to the Pima County Medical Examiner's office in Tucson for an autopsy. We have a contract with them because Bisbee is too small to have our own medical examiner."

"How long do you think it will take to get results of the autopsy?" Cat asked. "And are we allowed to read the report?"

"No, these reports are not given to the public. I'll get a copy and read it so I'll be able to give you a general idea of what the medical examiner finds. As far as how long it will take, I just don't know. A day or two maybe. Pima County is big. They deal not only with dead bodies in the city, but also out in the county. That includes all those migrants who get lost and die in the desert. I'll call you when I know something."

"Meanwhile…," Cat hesitated, "I'm not sure what to do."

"Not much you can do at this point," Sam Morales said. "Mr. Trevelyan, will you be here for a while?"

"Yes. As you know, the intruder attempted to enter my room. I'll be here if there's another break-in. I want to make sure Cat stays safe until we get this resolved."

"That's good. I'll be going now. I'll call you when I know the arrival time of the crime scene investigation team. I don't need to tell you that no one should go into the gallery area. That includes you and Mr. Trevelyan."

"Believe me, I don't want to go in there," Cat said.

Miles nodded. "We'll shut the gallery off."

"Good. See you later," Sam Morales said. He rose and walked back to his squad car.

"I'm hungry," Miles said.

"I bought some homemade tamales," Cat said.

Miles nodded. He disappeared and returned ten minutes later with heated up tamales and a small salad for them both.

"I think maybe I'll try out some of the restaurants in Bisbee so I can identify good Sonoran cuisine cooks," Miles said as they ate. "Then I'll try the recipes in your kitchen. Maybe I could write a book about Sonoran cuisine. That sounds like fun, too."

"I think I'm not going to be of much help to you. I'm not a very good cook, and also I feel really distracted."

"Of course you do. After we eat, let's come up with a plan and conduct our own little investigation. I think your police are going to be focused on that dead body. We need to figure out who that intruder was and why he tried to break in."

"I think you're right about that," Cat said. "We could start with an inventory of the art, but we're not allowed into the gallery now or into our storage room either."

"Did Luis keep business records?"

"Yes. He told me once he kept them stored in Google Drive."

"Perfect," Miles said. "Storing everything in the cloud will make access easy. But only if he gave you access, too."

"I'm co-owner of everything. So yes, I have the option of going into his account there. It's under our gallery's name, Sonoran Art Gallery. I have the password somewhere. I'll have to find it."

"Maybe there will be something there that will tell us what the intruder was looking for."

Cat nodded. "Miles, there's something I forgot to mention. This morning people came to the gallery. First, there was a man who knocked on the front door glass. He said he was from Los Angeles and wanted to see the artwork of Jax Beringer. He seemed nice enough, rather friendly, so I let him in."

Miles frowned, "Cat, for the foreseeable future, I suggest you become less trusting of people who show up here with no notice."

"Does that include you?" she asked. She bit her lower lip so she wouldn't smile.

Miles looked at her in surprise. "Me?"

She couldn't help herself. She grinned. "I'm teasing you. Okay, I'll be suspicious and rough on everyone except my favorite clarinet player, the baronet Sir Miles."

Miles grinned. "Very good, m'lady. Keep in mind that I'm devoted to keeping you safe."

Cat smiled and squeezed his hand. "Anyway, this dude asked me something weird. He wanted to know if I had a watercolor done by David Hockney."

"He's a British artist."

"That's correct. Hockney lived in Los Angeles for years, then he went home to the U.K. His artwork is worth a bundle. There's no way we could have afforded any of his work. On top of that, our gallery has always only represented regional artists."

"So you have no idea why he thought you might have a Hockney?"

"No idea. That's not all. He looked at Beringer's big painting…"

"'Kissed'?"

"Right. He didn't look at anything else. He got all serious when he looked at the painting. Then out of nowhere, he asked if I wanted to sell the gallery to him."

Miles shook his head. "Very odd."

"There's more. This dude left, and not long after, a married couple showed up. They claimed to be from Bisbee. They got right to the point. They wanted to buy the gallery, too."

"They did? It seems strange to get two offers in one day, and your gallery isn't even for sale."

"That's exactly what I thought. The first guy's last name was Hubbard. The married couple's last name was Fuller. I forget their first names. The husband, Mr. Fuller, seemed pretty confident that I would change my mind. He's like those guys who always get their way. Like a boss in big business or something."

Miles nodded. "So there's something going on here behind the scenes. We'll look at Luis's papers for a start. Then let's go around and start asking people if anyone knows these people. I'm talking about Hubbard and the Fullers. Also let's talk to people about Jax Beringer. There may be a connection among all these people," he said.

Cat nodded. "I'm so glad you're here, Miles. I would be scared to death staying here alone."

"I'm pleased to be here as well, Cat. Don't worry. We'll figure it out. And we'll make sure you stay safe."

5 THE INVESTIGATION BEGINS

Later that afternoon, Cat said to Miles. "My computer isn't set up yet. I was going to put it on the desk in Luis's room. His laptop is in his closet."

"I have my laptop ready to go. Want to use it?"

"Will you sit with me, and let's take a look together at the gallery's files? Maybe you'll see something I don't."

"I'd be delighted to assist you, m'lady. Let's go to my room…or Luis's room."

"I'll go find my notebook with the password."

Ten minutes later, they sat shoulder to shoulder at the small desk in Miles's room. They began systematically going through a large file called "Sonoran Art Gallery." There were several smaller files contained in the big one. They found contracts with artists, photos with identification of individual artworks by size, medium, and subject, promotional material for the gallery and the artists, a record of exhibit openings and special shows, email lists of clients and potential clients, a collection of gallery newsletters, and even backup files for the gallery's website pages.

"Your brother was very well organized," Miles said as he turned to look at Cat. He gazed, lingering a moment on her face, then he turned back to his laptop. "Do you see anything unusual?"

"No. Even in the file labeled 'Watercolors,' there's no David Hockney. It's not there unless he hid it intentionally. But like I said, we only represent artists from this region."

"Let's take a closer look at the file for Jax Beringer."

As they perused the individual documents, they found information in the Beringer files organized in the same manner as other artists represented by the gallery.

"Look at this," Miles said. He pointed to a file folder.

Cat opened a file folder labeled "Contract Dispute." "Our attorney Jeremy Flores mentioned this. Jeremy told me that Beringer was contesting his contract with the gallery. Beringer wanted to go solo. We thought that he had plans to establish himself in New York City and get rich. Luis mentioned this to me, but he wasn't too concerned. He said the contract was legitimate, and it would be hard, if not impossible, for Beringer to get it nullified. The bastard was so ungrateful. Luis was responsible for all his success."

"And you, too. Shall we take a look at Luis's personal files?"

Cat grimaced. "That seems like an invasion of his privacy."

"Yes, but if he were here, I'm sure Luis would want us to do everything we could to figure out what is going on and to make sure you stay safe."

She nodded. "Yes, my big brother would want me to be safe."

Miles systematically opened the other folders. They found files similar to those of the gallery. There were personal tax forms, credit card bills, and operator's manuals for everything from the refrigerator downstairs to the computer itself. The only difference was a folder full of scanned print and digital photos organized by year.

"Very good. Family photos. Hey! Let's see if we can find you." Miles clicked until he found childhood photos of Cat, one with her mother, several of her with Luis, and some of her alone. One showed her in a softball uniform, and in another, she was in a ballerina's tutu.

"Oh, what's this?" He pointed to a photo of Cat as a teenager. She was dressed in a knee-length white nightgown. She was wearing heavy, dark combat boots. Her hair was dyed purple, and it stuck out in spikes all over her head. Bracelets covered one forearm from wrist almost to her elbow. Miles could see the upper edge of a tattoo on her left breast.

"That's me about to leave for the senior prom. I was kind of a wild child when I was in high school," Cat said. "I wrote bad poetry, and I was in a rock band for a while. I sang. I was bad at that, too."

"You were an adorable wild child. Very pretty." He turned and smiled at Cat.

Cat was staring at him, and for a long moment, she couldn't look away. Miles really was handsome, she decided. Not in a conventional, pretty boy, movie star way but different, solid, in a grown-up, real man kind of way. That strawberry blond hair, his fair complexion, his blue eyes, and broad shoulders all added up to a very attractive man. She wondered if he had a girlfriend back in England.

Miles spoke first. "Your eyes are a beautiful, rich brown color."

"Your eyes are very blue. And beautiful."

He turned slightly pink and looked away.

"Oh, look at that. I made Sir Miles blush." Cat giggled.

"You don't know how happy it makes me to hear you laugh," Miles said. He was looking at her again. "How old are you?"

"I'm twenty-seven. And you?"

"The same. Twenty-seven." He paused. "Twenty-seven has been a good year for me."

They both fell silent, smiling at each other.

"Are you married?" Cat asked suddenly.

His eyebrows went up in surprise. "No. I almost got married last year, but we decided that we were just getting married because all our friends were getting married. I still feel a lot of affection for her, and she for me. But we never really loved each other."

"What's her name?"

"Gracie. Well, really Grace, but everyone calls her Gracie."

"Is she still your girlfriend?"

"No. We parted ways before I left for America. She's gone off to South Africa to do research."

Cat smiled and returned her gaze to the computer screen.

"And you, m'lady. Are you married or do you have a boyfriend?"

Cat looked at him again. "No and no. I used to be married. Just after I got my university degree, I was hired by this company in Phoenix. So I moved to Phoenix and started working in the graphic design department. Not long after, I married this real jerk who worked for the same company but in a different department. I was young and naïve, and I didn't know what I was getting into. He was manipulative and demanding. Luis tried to warn me, but I didn't listen. We were married for two long, miserable years. Almost from the beginning, my husband was emotionally abusive. I spent most of my time trying to keep him from going off the rails and raging about some insignificant thing or other. He started pushing me around. That made me really scared of him. I thought he was going to beat me. When I filed for divorce, he caused a lot of trouble because he couldn't accept it. I had to get a restraining order against him because he was stalking me. We've been divorced for two years now, and he still bothers me sometimes. He's one of the reasons I decided to move home to Bisbee, to get away from him. I decided to stay away from men for a while. I get too easily confused."

"Confused?"

"I confuse lust with love."

Miles chuckled. "That's a very human problem. I think that's a good description of my relationship with Gracie. Lust but not love."

Cat nodded.

He turned back to the laptop. "This all looks pretty normal. So what's our strategy now?"

"Well, I was thinking that maybe we could just go around and chat with people. Maybe we can see if anyone can tell us anything about Beringer, like who might have had a conflict with him and who might have wanted him dead. Mainly, though, we need to figure out if there's a connection between the body in the wall and the intruder who came in last night. I really don't know why that man tried to break in."

"Right. We don't have enough information at this point."

"That reminds me. I need to find a handyman to come and install one of those metal screens on the glass door that goes out to the deck in your room. You can close it at night and not worry about anyone getting in, but you'll still be able to keep the glass open and freeze to death if you wish. I'll make a call and arrange that. Then we'll go around pretending we're just out having fun, and we'll ask a few questions in the process."

"I won't freeze. And instead of pretending, perhaps we might actually have fun."

Cat smiled. "Okay. I'm going downstairs and find my phone."

She returned a few minutes later. "I called Eric. He said he knows a lot of guys doing handyman work, but he suggested I try out a handywoman. He said she's young, and she wants to get established, but a lot of people are skeptical that she can do the work. Her name is Mari Spencer. I couldn't resist the idea of hiring a woman so I called her. She'll be here tomorrow in the late afternoon. The body should be gone by then."

Miles turned off his computer.

"Okay," Cat said. "Let's pretend we're Miss Marple and Sherlock Holmes, and go do some sleuthing."

"And have some fun, too."

* * *

Cat locked up the house and they departed through the back door.

Miles took her hand as they walked toward central Bisbee.

"Where shall we go first?" he asked.

"To my favorite bar. Bartenders hear a lot of talk. They usually know what's going on. This particular bar has a very well-informed bartender. And you'll like the beer."

They sauntered along holding hands until they came to the central business district. Cat led Miles up a second street to the north.

"This is Brewery Gulch. We're going to the Star Tavern." She pointed to the bar.

"Interesting name," Miles said.

They entered the tavern which was dark except for daylight coming from a narrow window high on the front wall and Christmas lights strung around the room near the ceiling. There were lights, too, behind the bar and over a pool table at the back of the room. Tables and chairs, mostly empty, were scattered throughout the room, and there were stools along the length of the bar. They could see a young woman with shoulder-length blonde hair standing behind the bar smiling at them. She lifted a short white towel from her shoulder.

"I was beginning to think no one in this town was thirsty," she said. "You're my first customers since lunch."

"It's a little early, Amanda, but we're ready for a drink. First, I want to introduce my friend Miles Trevelyan. He's here visiting for a couple of weeks. Miles, this is Amanda, and she's the proprietor of this establishment."

"Hi. It's a pleasure to meet you. I notice your pub has the same name as a famous pub in London," Miles said.

"Yes. I've heard of the Star Tavern. I hope to go there someday. You'll notice that I have an accent by way of Savannah, Georgia. You have an accent, too. Where are you from?"

"I'm English. From Sussex in the U.K."

"Excellent. I guessed that. What can I get for y'all?"

"I'll take a glass of red wine," Cat said. She looked at Miles.

"My favorite is a Scottish stout, but I doubt you have that so I'll take a Guinness. Do you have Guinness?"

"Yes, but try me on the stout. I'm going to guess Belhaven."

Miles gasped and grinned. "You have Belhaven? Yes, please. I'll take a Belhaven Scottish stout."

"Ale from the U.K. just happens to be our specialty. We have Guinness, of course, and a fine selection of bitters and stout, English, Irish and from Scotland, too. It's a little more expensive than what you're used to because we have to import it, but worth it when you're far from home."

"I think I'm in heaven. Thank you for bringing me here, Cat."

Amanda turned and retrieved their drinks. She placed Cat's glass of wine and Miles's beer before them on the bar.

"Amanda, we're here for something else, too," Cat said. "But you have to keep quiet and not tell anyone you've talked with me. I want to ask you some questions because I know you hear a lot."

"That's true. Like I know someone tried to break into your house last night, and y'all found Jax Beringer's body behind your gallery wall this morning." She grinned.

Now it was Cat's turn to gasp. "Where'd you hear all that?"

Amanda shrugged. "I have my sources. You know how Bisbee folks like to talk."

Cat shook her head. "We don't know for sure it was Jax Beringer."

"Just looks like him, huh?" Amanda chuckled.

"Yes. It's a brown skinned, shriveled-up dead body that looked like Beringer," Cat wrinkled her nose. "The forensic team is supposed to come tomorrow morning, and then the funeral home people will take him away to the medical examiner for an autopsy."

"Bisbee is usually pretty dull when it comes to crime, Miles," Amanda said. "What's happening now is kind of exciting and scary at the same time. You should know that I love mystery novels and read them all the time. So I'm all in on this real, authentic mystery, and I definitely want to help. What do you need to know?"

Cat sighed. "We're not sure where to begin. We'd like to figure out who broke into my house last night. There could be a connection between that and Beringer's body. Or not."

"The goal at every step is to keep Cat safe," Miles said firmly.

Amanda nodded.

Cat continued, "Here's a couple of facts. Beringer was trying to break the contract with our art gallery when he disappeared. This morning I had two offers to purchase the gallery. And one of those guys wanted to know if I had a David Hockney watercolor. That's very unusual. We have to do an inventory, but it's highly unlikely that we have a watercolor by Hockney."

"Who asked to purchase the gallery?"

"The first man said he was from LA. I remember his name now. Freddy Hubbard."

"As far as I know, he hasn't been in here. But I'm friends with a lot of the folks who work for local hotels. I'll see if I can get any info on him. He's very likely staying at one of the hotels or a bed-and-breakfast."

"Then there was a married couple named Fuller."

"Yes, I know Nolan Fuller. He comes in alone and drinks alone. He rarely says anything to me or anyone else. His wife, Helen, has never been in here. I'll ask around and see what people know about them."

"Okay, how about Jax Beringer?" Cat asked.

"How much time do you have? I know a lot about him. He is …or was… a real dick," Amanda said. "Do either of you have a notebook? You can make a list of all the people he's screwed over and who hate him. It's going to be hard to figure out who killed him because there are so many suspects."

Miles pulled a small notebook and a pen out of his pocket. "Ready," he said.

"First, does anyone suspect your brother? I know about the contract dispute," Amanda directed her question to Cat.

"No," Cat responded. "Luis was pretty chill about the contract because he said Beringer had no chance of breaking it. We think we've established that Beringer was killed during the time when Luis was really sick, and I was here at that time, too. We think he was killed somewhere else and his body stuffed into the gallery wall when I was in Phoenix getting my things to move back home."

"Okay. So let's talk about *friends* of Jax Beringer," Amanda sarcastically emphasized the word 'friends.'

She looked at Miles's empty glass. "Want another?"

"Sure," Miles looked at Cat. "You'll carry me home if I get a bit sozzled?"

"No!" She shook her head. "I can't carry you. You're bigger than me. And you told me that you would behave." Her lips twitched trying not to smile.

"Yes, I did say that," Miles frowned. "I'm beginning to regret that." He turned to Amanda. "Okay. Just one more pint. I can't resist. American beer is bloody awful. Mexican beer isn't much better. It's all lager." He made a face.

Amanda laughed. She poured Miles another glass of his favorite Scottish stout. "Need a refill on that wine, Cat?"

Cat shook her head no. "I don't want Miles to have to carry *me* home."

"Actually I think I might like that," Miles said.

Amanda continued. "Beringer was what we call a 'player.' He was very arrogant and just assumed every woman would want him and cave in to his advances. If a woman resisted, word is that he got aggressive and insisted."

"Yeah," Cat said, "he hit on me. Unsuccessfully. He got the message."

"Me, too," Amanda replied. "Also unsuccessfully. I could see right away that he was a user. The point is that there's a long list of women and even teenage girls who got used by him. I'll have to think about it to come up with a list of local names — there are so many — but it won't be comprehensive because he also had relations with women who were just here as tourists or to attend one of the festivals."

She took her towel and absentmindedly wiped the bar.

"The worst case I've heard of, though, was that he raped a young Mexican-American girl, just sixteen years old. She lives out at Double Adobe east of Bisbee with her mom. She worked after school cleaning houses. I don't know how she got on Beringer's radar. But word is that he hired her to clean his house then insisted that she have sex with him. When she resisted, he raped her. Her family talked about pressing charges, but Beringer laughed it off, saying that no one would believe a poor, young Mexican-American girl's word against his. He was, after all, a prominent, affluent, respected and *white* member of the Bisbee community."

Miles asked, "Do you know the young girl's name?"

"No, but I can find out."

Miles shook his head. "I don't like this man Beringer."

"Also there are a bunch of tradesmen he screwed around. I don't mean sex. I mean money screwed around. He thought he could get people to fix things for him for free or really low cost."

"No one tried to sue him?" Cat asked.

"Usually it worked the other way. He would file lawsuits. People here don't usually have enough money to hire a lawyer and defend themselves, much less sue him first, even when they are in the right."

Amanda listed off several people who had been in legal squabbles with Beringer. An auto mechanic, an electrician, Cat's plumber Eric Carter, four different carpenters, one of whom was Mari Spencer.

"Hey, she's coming to work on fixing my wall tomorrow," Cat said.

"That's good news. I had a conversation with her once. She's young and enthusiastic about her work. When she graduated from Bisbee High, she decided she didn't want to go to college or get some shit job here. So she enrolled in Cochise College and earned a certificate in what they call "Carpentry Technology." Mari is well trained. But right away, she bumped up against sexist prejudice against women doing that kind of work. She still struggles to get regular paying gigs. I'm really glad you're giving her a chance."

During this conversation, Miles was scribbling in his notebook.

"Also Beringer got into it with two of his neighbors over property rights, what could be planted here and there, parking, and noise. He was making the noise, not the neighbors. He sued them for harassment."

Cat remarked, "I'm glad I never had to deal with this *pendejo*."

"There are more incidents, too. I mean when you first met him, he'd pour on the charm. But not long after, you'd find he would want something from you and if you didn't give it to him right away, then he'd come after you. He made noises once about suing me for giving him bad beer."

Miles laughed. "What a tosser! This is the best pint I've tasted since I've been in the States. Or in Mexico, too."

"Thank you, Mr. Trevelyan." Amanda smiled in a flirtatious way.

Cat frowned when she saw this. She felt this little bite of jealousy. At the same time, she thought that it made no sense for her to feel this way. Miles wasn't her boyfriend. And he was leaving soon. She mustn't forget that. He was leaving.

"Oh, and some friends of his came to visit and stayed at the Copper Queen Hotel. So Beringer threatened to sue the hotel for not providing what he called "decent rooms." The Copper Queen, can you believe that?" Amanda added. "He also threatened to sue another one of the hotels for the same reason. That hotel, since gone out of business, backed down under pressure and gave his friends free rooms."

Miles continued to write in his notebook.

"And there are the folks at the bookstore, the ceramics store, and a couple of the restaurants. He even got into it with the librarian at the public library." She reeled off more names for Miles to write in his notebook.

"So he was generally unpopular?" Miles asked.

"Very unpopular," Amanda said, "among the locals, I mean. Tourists were impressed by him and what they considered his charm. Want another stout, Miles?"

"No, best not. Cat said she doesn't want to carry a drunken Englishman back to her home."

"Three pints make you that drunk?" Amanda said dubiously.

"No, but three makes me suffer the illusion that I can really handle four and then five and top that off with six. So I end up drinking more than I should, and before you know it, I'm legless."

"You mean you have trouble walking?" Cat asked.

"Something like that. I become rather helpless."

"Somehow I can't see you as ever being helpless," Cat said.

Miles answered in a serious tone, "I don't want to get drunk because I want to make sure you stay safe."

Amanda grinned. "Got yourself a real prince there, Cat."

"No, he says he's a baronet. I'm not really sure what that is exactly," she answered, "but he's a sweetheart, and he kept me from being hurt last night."

Miles was grinning now.

Amanda's gaze went back and forth between Cat and Miles. She smiled.

"Yeah, I see. I see what's going on," Amanda paused. "Well, that's all I have for you now. I'll text you when I have more info. So carry on, my friends."

Miles and Cat finished their drinks and said goodbye to Amanda.

Just as they opened the front door to leave, Miles turned and called to Amanda, "I'll be back for more of that Belhaven."

Amanda smiled and waved goodbye.

6 Questions

Cat and Miles headed back toward the curving main street that ran through Old Bisbee.

"What's next?" she asked.

"It's time to eat. May I take you to dinner?"

"What about all that food at home?"

"Tomorrow. We'll deal with that tomorrow. I'm hungry now. Starving really."

"Then let's see that you get to eat. Is there a restaurant or café on that list that Amanda gave you?"

"Yes, there are a couple places." He was looking at his notebook. "How about Jillie's Café?"

"Good choice. I know Jillie. Not well, but she's always been friendly to me."

"Let's go there. What kind of food do they have?"

"I think it's a vegetarian and vegan restaurant. That means lots of fresh vegetables and fruits. No meat."

"Anything Mexican? I mean Sonoran?"

"Probably. You can't get away without having something Mexican in this town. And the Mexican food here is all Sonoran."

They easily found the café, and, within minutes, they were checking out the menu.

"Oh, look! Vegetarian empanadas. That sounds good. Also there are a lot of native plants they offer. Nopal? That's a cactus, isn't it? They eat cactus?" Miles made a face.

"Yes, nopalitos. The cooks get rid of the spines first, so don't worry about that. I see here you can get chopped nopalitos and onions mixed in with scrambled eggs, or a bean dish, two types of beans, with tomatoes, onions, garlic, cilantro, and some peppers. They both sound good."

"What do nopalitos taste like?"

"Some people think like okra and others think green beans. To me, I just think they taste like nopalitos."

"Okay. I'll try it. Let's get both dishes and trade bites."

A young man in an apron came and took their order.

Before he left their table, Cat said, "Is Jillie here? I need about five minutes of her time."

The young man nodded, "I'll tell her."

A few minutes later Jillie appeared. She was a forty-something, very slender brunette with big, dark-rimmed glasses, a white cap on her head and a white apron. Her smile grew when she saw Cat. She leaned down to give Cat a hug.

"Hey, girlfriend! I heard you were coming home. Glad to see you."

"You, too, Jillie," Cat gestured to Miles.

"This is Miles Trevelyan. He's visiting from the U.K., and he's interested in Sonoran cuisine."

"Well, hello! You've come to the right place."

"Yes, thank you. Very shortly I will eat my first cactus."

Jillie grinned, "Nopalitos!" She sat down at their table.

Cat explained why she and Miles wanted to talk to her.

"Yeah, I heard about your break-in and about finding Jax's body in the wall of your gallery. Jax had a lot of enemies. Sorry to say this about another human being, but I think the world is a better place without him. My guess is that someone finally lost control and killed him in a fit of rage. As far as who that might be…," she shrugged her shoulders. "Frankly, I was surprised not so much that he had been murdered, but more about his body being found in your gallery wall."

"Have you heard about any fairly recent conflicts he had with anyone?"

"Seems like there was always something," she paused. "Back in the summer, Jax got into it with someone doing carpentry work on his house. I can ask around and see who knows what that was about. But that's just the most recent. He frequently had disputes with workmen. He didn't want to pay them."

Jillie turned to Miles and smiled, "So what brings you to this part of the world, Miles? Do you like our food?"

Was Jillie batting her eyelashes? Cat felt herself getting annoyed again. Is every woman in Bisbee going to flirt with Miles Trevelyan?

"Yes, I'm a big fan of Sonoran cuisine. But I'm here because I'm a scholar. I'm doing research for a new book about the Borderlands," Miles answered. He returned Jillie's smile. "Don't allow me to interrupt you. Please continue, Jillie."

"Well, you probably know about that young Mexican-American girl who worked as a maid. Jax got her pregnant, and she just recently had the baby. Some people say he raped her. I wouldn't be a bit surprised if that's true. I heard that she and one of her brothers went to him to try to get some financial support for the baby. Jax laughed her off. He insulted her by saying that she was a get-around girl, and the baby could be anybody's. She went away empty-handed. I heard that the brothers were really pissed. She has two brothers. It's possible that one of them or someone else in her family decided to confront him. Maybe things got out of hand. But why put his body in the gallery wall? That's a little weird."

"I agree," Cat said. "If someone got in an argument with Beringer and killed him, accidentally or intentionally, sticking the body in the wall of the gallery makes no sense. It would have been easier to take the body out in the desert somewhere and dump it."

"Any idea why someone would want to break into Cat's gallery?" Miles asked.

Again, Jillie shrugged. "Burglary would be my guess. Unless the person who tried to break in was the same one who put Jax's body in the wall."

Miles and Cat looked at each other. "I never thought of that," said Cat.

"Got to get back to work," Jillie said. "I'll let you know if I hear anything. Come back anytime, Miles. You, too, Cat." She returned to her kitchen.

"Your fellow townspeople are very well-informed," Miles said.

"Yeah, Bisbee is totally into gossip."

"So a get-around girl is one who has sex with different blokes?"

Cat nodded. "Yes. In this case, I doubt that she was like that. She was so young. Most likely, she was a virgin."

As they were finishing their meal, the waiter appeared with a jar of jam and some toast.

"Compliments of Jillie," he said.

Cat smiled. "Here's another use of nopal cactus. This jam is made of the fruit of the nopal. The fruit is called 'tuna.' Try it."

He spread some of the jam onto the toast. "Hmmm….this is excellent. Very sweet taste. You are opening new culinary doors for me, m'lady."

Miles's cell phone played a soft melody. He pulled it out of his pocket and looked at it. "A text from Amanda. She says the man who made you an offer to buy the gallery, Freddy Hubbard?" He looked at Cat and she nodded.

"Amanda thinks he gave you a false name. There's a guy staying at Hotel Tranquilo who matches his description. His real name is Freddy Howard. Or that's the name on his credit card. He's from Los Angeles."

"Curious. Why would he give me a false name?"

Miles shrugged. "I don't know, but I think it might be a good idea to find out as much as we can about Freddy and also about Jax Beringer. He had a life before he came to Bisbee. All this trouble may be about something that happened before he even arrived here. Let's find out more about these blokes."

"Then maybe we can talk to him directly. But first I need to make a pit stop. I mean I have to go to the ladies' room."

"I'll wait here for you, and then I'll go to the loo, too. I think I drank too much ale."

Cat disappeared for a few minutes. Then Miles went.

Cat sat waiting at their table, watching people go into and out of a market in the alley across the street between two red brick, two-story buildings. Vendors' tables were set up along both sides of the walkway. She could see both arts and crafts vendors and a couple of people selling fresh vegetables. Several people had big shopping bags or baskets. Nearly everyone was smiling.

Cat realized that she felt like herself for the first time in a while. She was relaxed, and she felt safe. She could thank Miles Trevelyan for her sense of safety. On top of all that, she was really enjoying his company. He was interesting and funny and nice to look at, too. She looked forward to spending the evening with him.

Suddenly everything changed. A thin man with scraggly, shoulder-length hair appeared on the sidewalk just in front of the restaurant. He moved his hand up against the front glass and peered into the restaurant.

Oh, no! Cat's body stiffened. The man was her ex-husband, Al Kemp. What was he doing here? she asked herself frantically. She could see the frown on his face and his jerky, impatient movements. She knew right away what he wanted. He was looking for her. Her relaxed state turned instantly into intense anxiety. She rose and turned, hoping to go out the back door of the restaurant before Al could see her.

Too late! He slammed open the door of the restaurant.

"There you are!" he said in a loud voice. "I've been looking for you everywhere. Come here, Cat," he demanded.

Before Cat could take even a step away from her table to escape his grasp, Al moved forward quickly and grabbed her wrist.

"I said, 'Come here!'" He jerked her toward him violently and pulled her out onto the street. She pulled against him, but he was stronger and angry, too.

At just that moment, Miles reappeared and saw Cat being man-handled. He ran forward and went through the restaurant door just in time to see this strange man pulling Cat away. He could see her resisting, pulling against the man, and yelling, but she wasn't strong enough.

"Let me go, Al!" she cried. She stumbled.

Before she could hit the concrete sidewalk, Miles was there catching her and pulling her to her feet. At the same time, he grabbed Al's arm and twisted it so that Al was forced to relinquish his grip on Cat's arm.

Cat saw the two men look at each other in the eye. "Murderous" was the word that popped into her head when she saw Al's face. She froze. Then she looked at Miles. He was calm as ever with an impassive look on his face.

"Leave the lady alone," Miles said. His voice was quiet but commanding.

"Get lost!" Al yelled. "She's my wife!"

"I'm *not* your wife, Al. Just leave me be. Go back to Phoenix, and let me become a memory." She was close to tears.

"I won't let you go, Cat. You don't belong here in this godforsaken little town. You belong with me. You have to come back to Phoenix with me."

"*No!*" Cat cried.

"The lady said 'no," Miles said.

Al glared at Miles. Then he rushed forward and smashed into Miles who lurched backward but managed to stay on his feet.

Seeing that, Cat felt this intense burst of rage. How dare he hit Miles like that? She picked up a nearby chair at one of the restaurant's outdoor tables. She swung it hard against Al's shoulder and head. Al yelped and swerved away.

Miles moved toward Al who came at him again. Al threw a punch. Miles easily ducked out of the way, and Al's fist hit thin air.

Miles responded with his own punch which landed squarely against Al's nose and mouth. Al went down hard on the concrete. He sat up, his hand to his now-bloody nose.

"Who the hell are you?" Al demanded of Miles.

"I am Miles Trevelyan. I am here to protect and care for Ms. Miranda."

Cat came to stand next to Miles. She glared at Al.

Al was on his feet now. His entire body was tense and twitching with fury.

"Stop immediately!"

The sudden sound of Bisbee police chief Sam Morales ordering them to stop fighting got their attention. Sam Morales had been driving up the street when he saw Al pull Cat out of the restaurant. Morales pulled over and turned on the revolving lights of his patrol car as he watched Miles and Al trade punches. The he called out using his PA system.

"I told you to stop!"

Morales got out and approached. "What's going on here?"

Cat spoke first. "This is my ex-husband. He's wants to force me to return to Phoenix. I don't want to go."

"And Trevelyan here was attempting to render aid?" Morales asked.

"That's correct, Officer," Miles said.

Morales turned to Al. "What is your name?"

"Al Kemp. Cat is my wife."

"*Ex-wife!*" Cat said vehemently. "We've been divorced for two years. He won't leave me alone. I had to get a restraining order against him in Phoenix."

Morales turned back to Al Kemp.

"I saw you assault and attempt to kidnap Cat Miranda. I saw you assault Miles Trevelyan. I could arrest you and take you in right now. But I'm going to make it easy on you by giving you a choice, Kemp. You get in your car and drive out of Bisbee immediately. Never come back here. Understand? Your other option is to be arrested for assault and attempted kidnapping."

"I'm leaving," Al growled.

"Good. Get out of town now, and don't come back," Morales said. "And if I ever see you in this town again, I will arrest you immediately."

Al turned and stomped away. He went to a car parked about a half a block away, got in, and drove away toward the west. He was driving too fast, tires squealing.

"Thank you so much, Sam," Cat said.

Miles nodded. "Yes, thank you."

Morales said, "Just doing my job. Let me know if he shows up again. I mean it when I say I'll arrest him. I saw the entire incident. He started this."

Miles turned to Cat. "Are you hurt?"

"No. Thanks to you, I'm just fine," Cat smiled. "How about you, Miles?"

He looked at his hand. "Perhaps some skinned knuckles. It's nothing."

"I bet that stings. Come on. Let's go home, and we'll fix you up."

They said their goodbyes to Morales and set off walking west along Tombstone Road toward Cat's home.

"You're quite good at throwing a chair," Miles said.

"Thanks." Cat slipped her arm in his. "You're good at throwing a punch."

"I didn't want him to hurt you."

"You're so fine," she said, looking up at him with a smile. Cat took her arm from his and put it around his waist. She was thinking about how Miles told Al that he was there to protect and care for her. She liked that a lot.

"Thank you, m'lady." His arm went around her shoulders. Miles grinned.

* * *

They arrived at Cat's home just as the sun was starting to go down. Miles went around the lower floor and then the upper to make sure no one had attempted to break in while they'd been gone.

He returned to the kitchen. Cat was making hot tea.

"Let me take a look at your hand."

"I washed it upstairs in the bathroom. It's clean. No need for a bandage. It's only skinned."

"Then let's take our tea upstairs and do some searching on your computer," she suggested. He nodded and together they climbed the stairs.

Miles turned on the small table lamp so the room wouldn't become completely dark after the sun disappeared below the horizon. He turned on his laptop.

"Let's start with Freddy Howard," Cat said. Miles sat close to her as she used the mouse and keyboard to do a search. A long list of names showed up.

Miles shook his head. "Fred Howard, Freddy Howard, Frederick Howard. This could take a while."

"Los Angeles is a big city. And there are a lot of smaller cities in the LA area. Let's try Jax Beringer."

They spent ten minutes wading through media accounts of Beringer's art activities in the Los Angeles area. There were a couple of brief profiles of Beringer and reviews of his artwork. The profiles both had photos of Beringer.

"So that's what he looked like?"

They stared at the photo of Beringer. He was medium height with a wiry build, and dark hair pulled back into a pony tail at the base of his neck. He was smiling, but the smile did not reach his dark eyes.

"Yes. That's him. Do you think he looks like the dead body in my wall?"

"Yes, I do think so. I'm fairly sure that the body will be officially identified as Beringer."

Cat nodded and continued searching. She liked it that Miles was so close to her. Sometimes their shoulders touched.

As she searched, she found frequent press notices of Beringer's presence at a number of art exhibit openings, typically accompanied by at least one photo. Usually he was standing with a small group of people, all of whom were holding wine glasses and looking more than a little bored.

Then Cat and Miles hit pay dirt.

"Look," Cat said. She pointed at the screen where they could see a notice of an art opening. Two men were standing together. One of the men was Jax Beringer. The other man had his arm around Beringer's shoulders.

The caption read: "Pacific Palisades's Freddy Howard announced at the opening that he now represents artist Jax Beringer at his Art Pacifica Gallery."

"So they had a business arrangement," Miles said.

"Yes, but this was five years ago. Let's see if we can find something more recent."

She clicked on more links.

"Oh my god," she said.

The headline said, "Gallerist Freddy Howard and Artist Jax Beringer Married in Santa Monica." The article was a standard marriage announcement, and the photo showed both men in tux. Freddy was holding flowers, and Jax had a champagne glass in his hand. They were smiling.

"The date on this indicates they married four years ago."

Miles was smiling now. "Very interesting. So these blokes were married. That means they were gay, right?"

"Yes, looks like," said Cat. "I don't know what to think. Beringer had such a reputation with the women…."

"He was a get-around bloke. Maybe he both liked men and women."

"Big time get-around. As far as I know, he only showed interest in women in the time he's been in Bisbee. He came here about two years ago."

"Do you suppose these two are still married or are they divorced?"

Cat shook her head and shrugged her shoulders. "I really don't have any idea. But that may explain why Howard was looking for a Hockney watercolor."

"Right. Perhaps Howard owned it, and Beringer stole it. Or maybe they owned it jointly, and Beringer took it when he left Los Angeles. Or maybe it's Beringer's and Howard wants it."

"I don't know why he thought Luis might have it. Let's try to find Howard and see what he says."

"Okay."

"Do you think he might be the one who tried to break into your room?"

Miles shrugged his shoulders. "It was dark and the intruder was dressed in black with a mask. I can't say with any certainty."

"What do you think of the idea that the intruder might be the one who killed Beringer?"

"No way to know at this point. That's why we need to look into Beringer, too."

Cat looked at him and smiled. "Want to sit with me on the deck outside your room and relax a bit? Then I'm going to go to bed. I'm exhausted."

"I'd be delighted to sit with you. We can see the stars. They're very bright here."

Cat fetched a sweater from her room and put it on. They moved out onto the deck and relaxed into folding camp chairs.

Miles broke the silence. "Do you mind if I ask you some questions?"

"What do you want to know? I don't know very much."

"You never seem to give yourself enough credit. I think you know more than you realize."

She smiled. "Okay. Go ahead."

"As you know, I'm studying the history and culture of the Mexican and American border. You are very interesting to me because you seem to be a good example of a native of the Borderlands. You are culturally both Mexican and American."

Cat nodded. "That's true."

"So could you tell me something about your family? Did your family come from deeper in Mexico originally? Or are you descended from those Mexicans who were here all along? The U.S. bought this region in the Gadsden Purchase in the 1850s, and they found themselves suddenly living in the U.S., not Mexico."

"Yeah. There's a saying. It's something like 'We didn't cross the border. The border crossed us.' My mother's family is from Nogales, Arizona. That's the Mirandas. There are a bunch of Mirandas over there on both sides of the border."

"Ambos Nogales?"

"That's right. Ambos Nogales. Both Nogales, Sonora, and Nogales, Arizona. But to answer your question, we think the family came from further south originally. So let's start with two sisters. One is my grandmother Jimena, who died a few years ago. I always called her *abuela* which means 'grandmother.' Oh, but you know that because you speak Spanish," she smiled.

Miles nodded.

Cat continued. "My *abuela*'s sister, Luz Maria, is the grandmother of my cousins, the Nogales Mirandas. We also have more distant cousins in Sonora. The last I heard, Luz Maria's daughter and her two granddaughters live in Nogales, Arizona. Her grandson moved to Tucson recently. His name is Francisco Miranda, but we call him Frankie. Once I asked my mom about that side of the family, and she told me that the Mirandas originally came from the state of Sinoloa. Do you know where Sinoloa is?"

"Yes, the state just south of Sonora, along the Pacific coast."

"So there are probably Mirandas there, too, but I don't know them."

"Why did this branch of your family come north?"

"I don't know, Miles. Luis and I talked once about doing a family history, but we never got around to it. He loved history."

Cat fell silent for a few minutes. Just mentioning Luis's name made her sad.

"I know absolutely nothing about my father. Luis and I both tried to get my mom to tell us something, but she refused. In fact, she would walk out of the room if we started asking."

"Luis was a little older than you. Does he remember his early childhood, and about your birth?"

"Luis was five when I was born. He told me once that he could remember being on a ranch somewhere. He thinks it was in Mexico because everyone spoke Spanish. He is pretty sure that I was born in the U.S. because he remembers being in a big city and everyone speaking English. My birth certificate says I was born in Tucson. His says he was born in Nogales, Arizona. He thought maybe he was really born in Mexico and our mother claimed citizenship for him since she was a U.S. citizen. Or maybe she spent a lot of time in Mexico on a ranch somewhere, and she took him with her. We just don't know."

"Why do you suppose you and Luis both have your mother's surname?"

"I assume we are both illegitimate. I hate that word, by the way. What baby is ever illegitimate?"

"I agree."

"Neither of our birth certificates have a father's name."

"Do you think you both had the same biological father?"

"That's another thing we talked about. We figured if we got one of those DNA tests, we could find out. But it doesn't matter. He was my big brother."

Cat fell silent. She fought against tears.

"I'm sorry, Cat. Do you want to stop talking about this?"

"No, Miles," she said quietly. "I need to accept his death. Talking about Luis is a way to honor him."

He handed her his handkerchief.

"When I was really little, *mi abuela* took care of us when our mother was working. I think I told you she was a nurse at the Copper Queen Hospital in the Warren part of Bisbee. When I was about five and in kindergarten, *mi abuela* died suddenly of a heart attack. Luis was ten years old then. He stepped in to take care of me. We'd walk home together from school every day. Luis would get me a snack and help me with my homework. He played games with me, too, and taught me how to throw a ball. When we got older, he listened to me complain about school and friends, and he gave me advice. He was my big brother, but he was more than that. Our mother was good to us, but she was always a little distant. Luis was always there for me."

Miles listened quietly.

"Luis finished high school and went off to college. When our mom died in a car wreck, Luis came home, and I moved in with him. Then it was my turn to go off to college. I was almost seventeen when Luis took me in. Luis loved me a lot. He was the one I went to for everything. And now he's gone."

Miles nodded. "Yes, he loved you a lot. That comes through strong and clear."

"I don't really know what to make of these little surprises I'm discovering after his death. He left me the gallery as a viable business, a decent bank account, and property I didn't even know about until today. He's still taking care of me." She wiped tears away. "And now we've got this really bizarre situation with a body in the wall of the gallery. I don't know what to think. I wish he were here so I could talk to him about this."

"You can talk to me. But right now, you're tired, Señorita Catalina Amalia Miranda. Let's get some sleep. Tomorrow we'll take up this mystery again."

Miles pulled her up from her chair and held her hand as they walked to her bedroom door.

"Miles, can we keep our bedroom doors open tonight? I think I'll feel safer if I have to call you."

"Of course, m'lady. I'll be able to hear you more easily if you need me." He squeezed her hand.

Cat went into her room, and Miles went to his. Both doors stayed open.

7 Goodbye to Jax

The next morning began again with Cat and Miles making break-fast together. They went to the back porch to drink coffee.

"I received a text from Sam Morales," Cat said. "He says two crime scene investigators will be here by nine this morning. I'm supposed to be here to let them in. Then the funeral home guy is coming later." Cat paused. "I'm not sure what to do with myself. I can't do any work in the gallery."

"Want me to help you move the boxes into your room and help you unpack?" Miles suggested.

Cat scrunched up her nose. "To be truthful, I don't feel like doing anything."

"Then don't. Don't do anything at all. I just wish I could find a way to cheer you up a bit. I mean other than giggling every time you say 'Sir Miles.'"

"I don't." She smiled at him.

"Yes, you do. You think the whole idea of 'sir' is funny. I think you're a really cheeky girl."

"What does that mean?"

"Irreverent or even impudent. Or as you Americans put it, smart ass."

"*Not.*" Cat grinned.

"Too late. I've got your number, Miss Cheeky."

"You are aware, aren't you, that we had a revolution in 1776 to get rid of all the sirs and lords and ladies and dukes and all that foolishness."

"Yes, I'm aware that there was a significant status change in one of the Colonies around that time."

"Oh my. Status change? The Colonies?" Cat shook her head with mock dismay. "You're hopeless."

Miles reached out and patted her hand.

"How about if you tell me a joke?" she said suddenly.

"A joke?"

"Yeah, I bet you know some jokes. Tell me an English joke."

"Okay. How about this one? "Why is England the wettest country?"

"Who knows. Maybe the jet stream? I don't know. Tell me."

"Because the queen has reigned there for years."

Cat hesitated a moment, then she broke out laughing. "That's a terrible joke. Totally dumb. Almost as dumb as my joke about the elevator."

"Made you laugh," Miles said. He wiggled his eyebrows.

"That you did." She sat back in her chair.

"Later I'll make you some spotted dick," Miles said.

Cat's eyebrows went up. "*What*?" She giggled again.

Miles was grinning now. "Have you ever tasted spotted dick?"

"Is this some kind of dirty joke about a penis with freckles?"

"*No.*" He was laughing out loud now.

"Hey, I'm not entirely clueless. I've heard of spotted dick. It's something baked or fried, right?"

"Spotted dick is a pudding made with currants. You usually eat it with custard."

Cat shook her head and rolled her eyes. She was grinning. "You Brits are strange."

"I made you laugh. And I'll make you laugh some more. I think before recent events, your natural personality was to be fun-loving and to laugh a lot."

"Yes, that's what people have always said about me. I do like to have fun."

"Then let's bring that Cat back to life. The real you."

Cat nodded. "Yes, sir, Sir Miles." She giggled.

"See? You can't say 'Sir Miles' without laughing. By the way, do you Americans do knock-knock jokes?"

"Of course."

"Knock knock."

"Who's there?" Cat answered.

"You know!"

"You know who?"

"Exactly."

Cat groaned and laughed at the same time. "That's so bad."

Just at that moment, they both heard a vehicle coming up the street. It stopped in front of the gallery. Two doors opened and shut.

Cat immediately became serious again. "That must be them." She rose and went around the house to greet the crime scene investigators. Miles followed her. They found two men getting equipment out of the back of the van.

"Miss Miranda?" one of the men said. "We're here from Tucson to investigate the crime scene. I understand you have a dead body on the premises."

Cat introduced herself and Miles. "Come this way. I'll show you."

The two men followed her into the gallery. They both had on white jumpsuits and white protective nets on their heads. At the entrance to the gallery, they slipped blue cloth booties over their shoes.

Cat pointed to the hole in the wall. "He's in there."

From across the room, Cat and Miles watched them retrieve tools and begin their investigation. The men took photos, made measurements, dusted for fingerprints, and collected bits of mysterious substances that they put into small glass vials.

When it became apparent that they were going to be there a while, Cat said, "Miles, let's make a list of people that we want to track down and talk to about Jax Beringer."

"Good idea." He retrieved his notebook, and they went out to the back porch again.

"First, try to find Freddy Howard?" Cat asked.

"We can call Hotel Tranquilo and see if Hubbard is really Howard."

"We probably will have to come up with an excuse about why we're calling. I doubt they will just give that information out to anyone."

"Maybe the hotel will have someone on duty who knows you. You seem to know a lot of people."

"That's because I grew up here. People like Eric the plumber stayed after high school. Some of my classmates left and then returned, like me. Some left forever. Some like Amanda and Jillie are newbies who moved in, but they've been here long enough that a lot of people know them, including me. I bet we'll find several people who can help us."

"Next?"

"Track down some of the people who had conflicts with Jax Beringer?"

"And the girl who says Beringer is the father of her child," Miles added.

"Also, I'd like to know why those two people, the Fullers, want to buy this gallery. It just seems odd that they would show up all of a sudden. I understand why Freddy Howard might want it because he had a relationship with Beringer and because we have so many of his paintings in our possession now."

Miles nodded.

Cat stopped and shook her head. "I'm saying 'we' and 'our' as if Luis were still here. I'm alone now. The gallery is mine to deal with."

"I'm here, Cat. I'll do everything I can to help you."

She looked at him. "You won't be here forever, Miles." Cat felt an unexpected pang of sadness.

He frowned. "True. But I'll be here to help you get through the worst of this."

They fell silent for a while.

Cat spoke first. "When I talked to Jeremy, our attorney, he said we have to go through something called 'probate.' He said it would be easy because Luis left a good will. That means that someone will have to handle all that probate stuff for Jax Beringer now that he's dead."

"We have probate in the U.K., too. Probate deals with assets and also debts of the deceased."

"So first there will be the autopsy to prove that body is Beringer's. Then I'll probably need a lawyer to deal with Beringer's estate and the probate court. The gallery should be able to establish our legal right to maintain possession of Beringer's artwork and to continue to sell it. I can make sure that Beringer's estate will get its share of the art sales money."

"Jeremy Flores won't handle this for you?"

"He's up to his ears in work. He basically begged me to not give him any more work. I'll have to find another lawyer to deal with what comes out of the situation with Beringer."

"Perhaps this is a factor in Beringer's death," Miles said. "I mean what happens to his estate and his debts, too."

"Yes. Especially if he didn't leave a will."

The two crime scene investigators appeared at the back door.

Cat and Miles stood up.

"We're finished here. We'll be doing an analysis of evidence and writing a report. I've already called the funeral home to get someone in here to remove the body. I need to get your fingerprints so we can sort them out from anyone else in here. We have the plumber's prints already."

Cat and Miles submitted to having their prints taken.

"Thank you so much for coming early," Cat said. "This has been quite a shock. I'd like to get back to normal life as soon as possible."

"You should have your gallery back by the end of the day."

The two men left.

Cat called Hotel Tranquilo. Almost immediately, she was talking to someone she knew.

"Hey, this is Cat Miranda. How are you, Rick?"

There was a pause and then Cat explained that she was looking for Freddy Howard. "He came by the gallery and was interested in a couple of paintings. I'd like to connect with him again before he leaves town."

Another pause.

"Thanks so much, Rick. If you see him this afternoon, please tell him I'd like to talk with him about the art. I'll keep an eye out for him myself. See you soon!"

Cat looked at Miles. "Success! Let's hope Howard shows up here. If not, we'll go looking for him."

"Was that one of your old classmates you were talking to?"

"Yes," she paused. "Do you hear that? That must be the funeral director."

They both went around the front of the gallery to find a woman and two men getting out of a long black hearse. The two men went to the back and retrieved a gurney.

"Hi, Nancy!" Cat said. "I heard you took over your dad's mortuary."

"Hi Cat. Yes, Daddy retired last year, and I took over. It's great to see you, Cat. I heard you were moving back home."

Cat nodded. "Nancy Conway, meet Miles Trevelyan." She led them all into the gallery and pointed to the hole in the wall.

"He's in there. We all think the body is Jax Beringer."

"Yes, that's what I heard," Nancy said. The funeral home director approached the wall and peered in. "Yep, that's Jax."

"Did you know him?" Miles asked.

"Unfortunately," Nancy looked at Miles. "He was very charming. Very manipulative. Almost always got what he wanted, then he'd dump you. He left a trail of broken hearts behind him."

The way she said this and the look on her face told Cat that Nancy was one of those with a broken heart.

"We want to figure out why he ended up in my wall," Cat said.

Nancy nodded. "Yes, that's definitely unexpected." She gestured to the two men to get started. "Sorry to be rude, but I can't visit very much with you today. We have to take the body to Tucson to the medical examiner's office and then come back before it gets too late. So we've got a drive ahead of us. But you and I can catch up later."

By this time, her two employees had Jax's body out of the wall, covered with a tarp and strapped onto the gurney. They took it out to the hearse and loaded it into the back.

Just as Nancy was getting into the hearse, she turned to Cat. "Hey, are you going to participate in the Great Stair Climb this year? I definitely am. I've been practicing," she grinned.

"That sounds like fun," Cat said. "Maybe Miles will want to come along. We'll look for you."

They waved to each other as Nancy and her crew drove away.

Cat waved and whispered, "Goodbye, Jax."

"What's this about climbing stairs?" Miles asked.

"We have this really fun event every year. Tons of people come out for it. We run a course of four and half miles through Old Bisbee that follows curvy roads and staircases. Remember the staircases you saw when you were hiking on the trail above town?"

He nodded. "You mean you run up the staircases, too."

"Yes, nine staircases to be exact. There are over one thousand steps in all. It's a lot of work, but it's fun, too."

"I don't know. I'm kind of out of shape."

"Oh, come on. We'll have fun."

He shrugged his shoulders.

"Let's go sit on the swing. We can look it up on my phone. There are maps, too. And there's a craft beer festival at the same time."

They did just that, sitting shoulder to shoulder on the swing, as they peered at the phone.

"Oh, look at this map. This looks difficult!" Miles had a look of mock horror on this face.

"It's fun! Oh, come on, Sir Miles. Do this for me, and if you can't do it for me, do it for the Queen!"

"How can I resist? Yes, I'll run with you. And I'll do it for you, not the Queen. But can we have a rest along the way? And maybe we can try some of that craft beer?"

"Of course. Just don't be offended if I win." Her eyebrows went up. The look on her face was a challenge.

"You probably will beat me. I've been eating too much Mexican food on this trip and not running every day like I usually do." He stood up and started jogging in place.

Cat laughed. "Sit down, Sir Miles. I think you'll like the challenge. And we'll have fun. Later, we'll get you some of that Scottish ale you like so much so you don't have to drink our lager."

"Stout. It's a deal."

* * *

In the afternoon after lunch, Mari Spencer appeared driving a small pickup truck. She was a beautiful young woman, tall and slender, dressed in overalls, a long sleeve t-shirt, and wearing lightweight leather work boots. Her long sun-streaked brown hair was tied back into a ponytail. She was carrying a carpenter's tool box.

"Hi, Mari. Nice to meet you. I'm Cat Miranda, the one who called you. This is Miles Trevelyan. He's visiting from England."

"Thank you so much, Miss Miranda, for giving me a chance. A lot of folks think a woman can't do this kind of work."

"Women can do anything they want, in my opinion. I've heard you do a good job. And call me Cat."

Cat led Mari upstairs to the room occupied by Miles.

"As you can see, we had an intruder who tore off the screen and broke into this room. Miles scared him off. What we need is one of those metal security screen doors installed where the screen was. Then Miles can keep the glass door open and still have fresh air at night."

"This will be pretty easy, Cat. I have the metal screen door in my truck. I'll go down these outdoor stairs to get the door and bring it up this way."

It took Mari less than an hour to install the security screen door. She demonstrated the bolt lock to Cat and to Miles, too.

"While you are here, I have another job that needs being done, too."

"Sure," Mari said. Cat could see that she was pleased to be offered a second job.

Down they went to the gallery with Miles trailing behind. Mari was carrying her tool box.

Cat led Mari to the large hole in the wall. She looked at Mari and was surprised to see a look of distress or even dread on Mari's face. Cat wasn't sure.

"This is where they found Jax?" Mari said in voice barely above a whisper.

"Yes. The identity of the deceased hasn't been confirmed yet," Cat said. "But everyone who has seen the body and who knew Jax all think it was him. They've taken him to Tucson to the medical examiner's office to do an autopsy."

Miles spoke. "Miss Spencer, may I look at your tools? My grandfather was a hobbyist. I'd like to see if his English tools are like yours."

"Yes, of course." Mari turned her head and gestured to the tool box on the floor behind her.

When she did that, Cat saw tears in Mari Spencer's eyes.

"Did you know Jax?" Cat asked in a gentle voice.

"Yes."

Cat waited.

Mari looked at her. "We were lovers. Then he dumped me. I know I'll get over him someday, but I'm not there yet."

Miles was carefully looking at each tool in the box. He glanced up at Mari when she said she'd been lovers with Jax Beringer.

Cat nodded. "How long ago with this?"

"He ended our relationship about three months ago." Mari shook her head. "Look, I'm sorry. I didn't come here to burden you with my troubles."

She stepped back from the wall. "I'll take some measurements. Then I'll come back with supplies. You'll need some drywall, tape, paint and all that stuff." She was back to business now. "The plumber is finished?"

"Yes, and the crime scene investigators have been here, too."

Mari frowned. "I guess someone killed him."

"Looks like," Cat said, "and stuffed his body in my wall. I have no idea why."

Mari looked at her and shook her head. "A lot of people didn't like Jax. He was good to me…..until he wasn't."

Miles was on his feet now listening.

"So how about if I call you tomorrow and set up an appointment? That will give me time to get everything I need to fix this."

"Sounds good to me," Cat said.

Cat and Miles walked Mari to the door and waved as she drove away in her little pickup.

"So, Mr. Trevelyan, what were you looking for in Mari Spencer's tool box? Or was that a true story about your *abuelo*. I mean your grandpa."

"Actually that was true about my grandfather. He was an accountant for all his adult life. But he liked to make things with wood. Toys, especially. I benefited from his toy-making when I was a boy. He had a little workshop in the backyard of the house where he lived with *mi abuela*."

Cat grinned when she heard the Spanish word for grandmother, *abuela*. "I hope sometime you'll tell me about little Sir Miles," Cat said. Then she giggled.

"*See?* There you go again. Say 'Sir Miles' and you start laughing. Cheeky girl."

Cat punched him lightly on the arm. "What else were you looking for?"

"A tool with a round head and a notch in it. Jax had all those impressions on his body of such a tool."

"Did you find anything?"

"No. Mari's hammer is like any other, no notches, although it did look quite new. No wear at all."

"Interesting," Cat said.

"Okay. I'm going to go make you dinner now."

"Spotted dick?" Cat couldn't help herself. She laughed again.

"No, sorry. That's too time-consuming. Anyway, I'm here now, and I'm going to try to make something I've never made before. Chili rellenos."

"I love chili rellenos. But I think you want to make me chubby so I'll lose the stair climb race."

Miles shrugged his shoulders. "I'll be chubby, too."

They went the kitchen and cooked together.

After supper and cleanup, Cat said, "Let's go to my room and connect the television. We can watch a movie and pretend we have normal lives."

The television didn't take long to attach to the cable. Cat gestured to a small settee under a large window.

"Let's sit here." There wasn't much room on the settee, and they sat close together.

They watched a French movie, *Lost in Paris*. Both of them laughed out loud at comedic scenes in the film.

When the movie was over, Cat felt sleepy, but she didn't want to go to bed. She didn't want Miles to leave her room. She slumped in her seat and not long after, she drifted over until she was leaning again him.

"Time to go to bed, poppet," Miles said. He sat her up. "Ready?"

"Hmmm….," Cat said. She stretched and stood. "I'm sleepy. See you tomorrow, Miles."

"Until tomorrow." He left the door to her room open.

Miles went to his room. He left his door open, too.

* * *

Miles Trevelyan was quite aware that he really could be working on his laptop organizing all the notes, texts, correspondence and documents he'd collected in the past six months. When he needed a break from organizing, he could be wandering around this sweet little town with its steep canyon walls, curving streets and lovely old homes. He could be going across the border at Naco. He could be talking to people about the regional history. He could be doing what he came here to do. He could be. He could be.

But he couldn't. He couldn't bring himself to leave Cat. By now, Miles had to admit to himself that he was quite enchanted with the lovely Catalina Amalia Miranda. When she laughed, her entire face lit up, her dark eyes twinkled, and her cheeks turned pink. She was so warm when she fell against him on the settee. And when she was sad, it was all he could do to not take her into his arms and hold her. And kiss her. So warm. Her body was soft and curvy and….

Don't go there, Miles, he said to himself. Stop thinking with your knob. The term 'spotted dick' jumped into his mind. He laughed in spite of himself. He felt good. He had made Cat laugh more than once today.

8 Carmen

After breakfast, Cat said to Miles, "Are you sure you don't want to go work on your book? I feel kind of guilty that you are spending all your time on my problems."

"I can work on the book anytime. I'd rather be with you. Since we don't have to be here today, I suggest we gather more information."

Cat noticed what Miles had said. "Be with you." Just be with her. She felt warm all over. She knew in that moment that she just wanted to be with him, too, no matter what they did together. She smiled at him.

"I'll try Hotel Tranquilo again." She called the hotel, but Howard wasn't in, nor was her friend Rick.

"Let's see if we can track down that young girl who gave birth to the baby said to be fathered by Jax Beringer."

"Good idea. Do you think she'll talk to us?" Miles asked.

"I don't know. For a lot of women and girls, there's a lot of shame associated with an unwanted pregnancy because it means the girl had sex."

"Even if it's rape?"

"Yes. That's why a lot of women don't report the rape. They feel self-blame, as if they'd done something wrong and brought the rape on themselves. They feel ashamed."

"How do you know all this?"

"After I got divorced, I volunteered at a women's shelter when I lived in Phoenix. There were young girls there who had been raped. Some had been trafficked. That was really awful to hear about. Every single one of the girls blamed herself and felt shame."

"But they were victims of violence."

"True, but women aren't really supposed to be having sex. Rape is shameful. Having sex for fun is shameful, too. It's like that everywhere in the world and has been for centuries. I guess it's changing but really slowly."

Miles shook his head. "I've never spoken to a woman about this. Do you think all women feel shame when they have sex?"

"No. Women have always enjoyed sex although they rarely admitted it. Like I said, times are changing now. Some of us, and more and more of us, are what they call 'sex positive.' We have a healthier attitude toward sex."

"'Us'? Are you sex positive?" He smiled at her.

"Sir Miles! You're asking me such an intimate question," Cat laughed. "Oh, there I am again, laughing at 'sir.' Okay. Here's how it is with me. I've always been kind of carefree, but I was never a get-around girl. Not that I condemn get-around girls. A woman can do what she wants to do. No problem. I had a couple of lovers when I was in college before I got married. Not at the same time," she smiled.

Miles grinned at her. "But that would be okay with you. Two at a time?"

"Sure," Cat laughed. "In my case, both dudes were older than me. One got his degree and was hired by company in San Francisco so off he went. The other one was in ROTC. He went into the Marines. He's been deployed to Afghanistan three times already. I still write him occasionally. Then I had that dreadful marriage to Al. I guess if I feel any shame, it's because I married that man. He was such a huge mistake. I don't know what I was thinking." Cat shook her head.

"We all make mistakes," Miles said.

"I have trouble forgiving myself for that one." She paused. "Luckily, I've never been sexually assaulted like several of the women at the shelter, although I've known several dudes who got a little too familiar with me. I had to correct them. I've been celibate for more than two years now. But I think sex is a good thing, and it's nothing to be ashamed of. I mean we all get here because our parents had sex, right?"

"Right. I'm relieved to hear you were never assaulted."

"Lots of women are sexually assaulted, one in five. Actually a lot of men are assaulted, too, but they rarely talk about it. If anything, the shame for sexual assault is even worse for men."

Cat looked at Miles seriously now. "That's just one reason I'm glad you were here the night that the intruder broke in. I don't know what that man had in mind. I thought about what you said. I agree. It's very possible that it was me he was after."

Miles took her hand.

"So, yeah. This young girl may talk to us, and she may not. No way to know. I'll call around now and see if I can find out who she is and where to find her."

Cat called barkeep Amanda first. She explained what she needed and got the information quickly. She thanked Amanda and hung up.

"Jeez. Amanda knows everything about everybody. The girl's name is Carmen Fuentes, and she lives out in Double Adobe. I have directions to her house. She lives with her mother."

"Where is Double Adobe?"

"It's a settlement east of Bisbee, kind of halfway between Bisbee and Douglas, which is a little town right on the border. There's an elementary school at Double Adobe. Most of the homes are on fair-sized acreages, like twenty to forty acres."

"Let's go and see what we can learn. We can drive my rental car."

"Okay, but will you allow me to drive? We'll go over to Warren, and I'll show you where I grew up, my old school, the hospital, all that. If I'm driving, you can enjoy the view. And I won't have to worry about your driving."

"Hey!" Miles grinned. "I'm a good driver."

"I'm sure you are, but you Brits drive on the wrong side of the road."

He shook his head. "Wrong side? I don't think so. The 'other side,' maybe, but not the 'wrong side.' Anyway, yes, you can drive my rental."

"And on our way to Double Adobe, you can tell me all about *your* sex life."

"Nothing to tell." He handed her the keys to his car.

Cat looked at him. "Sir Miles has turned a shade of pink. Sir Miles is blushing. I think Sir Miles has plenty to tell." Cat was grinning now. They both got into Miles's car.

"I have spent most of my life in the library," Miles said, closing the car door behind him.

"I personally know two people who repeatedly had sex in the book stacks of the University library. They produced a baby nine months later. More goes on in libraries than most people know. And by the way, your face is bright red now. Okay, I'll let you off the hook. But you'll never convince me that you spent all your time in the library just reading books."

"Oh god, Cat. Stop torturing me. I promised you that I would behave. You're making it really hard." He groaned. "No pun intended."

Cat fell silent. She realized that most men would find this talk very provocative. What was she doing talking to him like that? How would he take this? He would get the wrong idea. Or would he? She had to admit to herself that she found Miles very attractive. Was she sending a message that she was interested in him sexually? Yes, she was interested. But no, better not send that message. Remember, Cat, he's leaving soon. You'll never see him again.

"Sorry, Miles. I'm out of line. I won't say anymore. I apologize."

Miles sighed. "Well, sometime I will tell you everything you want to know. Or I could show you." He looked at her and grinned.

Oh dear. Cat turned on the car's engine and backed out of her driveway.

"Now it's your turn to blush, Señorita Catalina Amalia Miranda." Miles laughed.

"Shut up!" She made a face at him as she headed east through the heart of Old Bisbee.

They fell quiet for a while.

"Tell me about your name."

Cat took a deep breath. She was glad he had dropped the whole sex talk. "You know Miranda is my mother's family name. Catalina is the name of the mountain range on the north side of Tucson. Santa Catalina Mountains to be exact. Amalia was my great-grandmother's name."

"I love your name. It's beautiful."

"What's your name?"

"Miles MacTavish Trevalyan."

"MacTavish?"

"My mum's side of the family is from Scotland."

"Scotland. No Mexicans in your family?"

"Sadly, no," Miles shook his head. He was smiling as if the idea of a Mexican in his family was amusing. "My ancestors never spent much time in Mexico."

By this time, they had entered Warren, one of the Bisbee satellite communities.

Cat drove slowly through the streets, passing by the Copper Queen Hospital and the high school. She finally came to an older home painted a pale sage green. A large mesquite tree was in the front yard. She parked across the street.

"So this is where you grew up?"

"Yes."

Miles looked at her. Cat had tears in her eyes.

"You're thinking of your brother?"

Cat nodded.

Miles handed her a handkerchief.

"You're going to run out of those things," she smiled as she wiped her eyes. "Okay, you've seen all of Warren's hot spots. Let's go to Double Adobe."

* * *

Following Amanda's directions, Cat and Miles found the house fairly quickly. It was an unassuming white frame home with a wide covered porch set back from the narrow paved highway. There were no other houses in sight. A pickup truck was coming toward them as Cat turned into the long dirt driveway.

A couple of dogs came forward and started barking. The pickup turned into the drive behind them and parked next to their car. Miles and Cat got out of the car. Two burly young Mexican-American men got out of their pickup and glared at Miles. The dogs stopped barking. Miles stayed standing next to the car, and Cat moved forward toward the porch. Before she could get there, an older woman opened the door and stepped out. The two brothers moved to stand near the steps just below the woman.

Cat greeted the woman and asked for Carmen.

"I am Carmen's mother. Why do you want to see her?"

Cat could see a teenage girl watching her from behind the sheer fabric curtains in the front window.

Cat told the woman a little about herself and then said, "Someone murdered Jax Beringer and stuffed his body into the wall of my gallery. An intruder broke into my house. I think someone is after me, and I don't know why. But I think there may be a link to Jax's murder. My friend and I," she gestured to Miles, "are asking questions hoping to learn more. I just want to stay safe. I need help. I'm hoping you can help me."

The older woman nodded. She opened the front door, and Carmen came out. She was holding an infant in her arms.

"What do you want to know?" Carmen's voice was soft. To Cat, she seemed timid and maybe a bit nervous.

"Do you know anyone who might have wanted Jax dead?"

"Yeah, us!" said one of the brothers.

"Why?"

Carmen looked at her brothers. She turned back to Cat and said, "I was working in Bisbee after school. I was hired to clean some hotel rooms. Jax came up to me and asked me to clean his house. He offered me twice what I was getting at the hotel. So I agreed. The next day, I went to his house."

She paused. She had turned pale.

"That *pendejo* forced her," one of the brothers growled.

Carmen nodded. "I tried to fight him off, but he was stronger than me. He tore my clothes."

She wiped tears away from her eyes. Her mother handed her a tissue and patted her on her shoulder.

"When I discovered I was pregnant, my brothers and I went to see him. We asked for recognition. We asked that the baby be recognized by his father. We asked for some financial help for the hospital bills. Not much. We didn't ask for much. But he gave us nothing. He laughed at us."

One of the brothers interrupted. "Yeah, the *pendejo* laughed at us. He claimed that Carmen had a lot of boyfriends, and it could have been anyone who fathered the child. And he claimed that she came on to him, that she wanted it. He said she asked for it."

Carmen shook her head. "I didn't. I didn't ask for it. He said no one would believe me if I claimed otherwise."

"I believe you," Cat said. "So he denied responsibility for the rape and for the baby, too?"

Carmen nodded. "Then he said something even worse. Jax told me that I should feel honored. He said he had created a painting for me. He said it was in your gallery. He said it was called 'Kissed' and that every time I look at it, I should feel grateful and honored that he gave me any attention at all."

Cat shook her head. "*Pinche pendejo*," she said.

"That's right," the first brother said.

Cat was disturbed now. The rape was bad enough. She was just a teenage girl. And this was the first time that Cat had heard an explanation of what the title of that painting meant.

"I'm just sorry it wasn't one of us that killed him," the other brother said.

Miles came forward at that moment. "The cops are investigating this. They will eventually figure out where and when Beringer was killed. I think you two will be on their list of suspects," he gestured to the brothers. "You best have a good alibi of where you were and what you were doing so that you don't get accused of the murder. And best not tell the cops that you wished him dead."

Both brothers were taken aback. They hadn't thought that they might be accused of the murder.

"Yeah, okay. We'll do that," one of them said. "We didn't kill him. And we don't want to be blamed for it."

"May I see your baby? Little boy or little girl?" Cat asked.

Carmen opened the blanket and turned toward Cat. She smiled, "He's a boy. I call him José."

"He's beautiful," Cat said, "*Muy guapo.*"

Carmen beamed.

Cat stepped back to stand by Miles. "This is a very sad story. But you've helped me begin to find a connection between my gallery and the death of Jax Beringer. I'm not sure what this all means, but Miles and I are going to find out. He's helping me to stay safe."

Miles nodded solemnly.

"Meanwhile, here's the good news. First, you have a beautiful, healthy little boy who has come from heaven to live with you."

Carmen's mother nodded and smiled. She made the sign of the cross.

"Second, there's something called probate or probate court. I don't know how it works exactly. But when someone dies, especially if they don't have a will, then the court does this probate thing. Anyone who has a claim on the estate of the dead person will get paid according to what they are owed. If you can prove

Jax is the father of this baby, then the estate should pay you child support."

Carmen and her mother gasped. The two brothers nodded solemnly.

Miles added, "That will mean a DNA test to verify that Beringer is the biological father of little José."

Carmen frowned. "Will this test hurt my baby?"

"No," Miles said. "It's easy. They will collect some of his spit. Easy."

"So what do we do?" asked one of the brothers.

"Let's stay in touch. Here's my card." She pulled a business card for the gallery from her shirt pocket and handed it to Carmen. "I have to hire a lawyer myself because I have to prove a claim on Beringer's estate. I have several of his paintings. Our gallery had a formal business relationship with him. My lawyer could be your lawyer, too, and make sure you get a good deal. We want your baby to have his fair share. We're going now. Thank you so much for the help."

"Oh, no. Thank you!" Carmen said. The brothers and the mother all nodded their heads in agreement.

"Let's go, Miles."

Cat and Miles got back in his car and drove back out onto the highway.

* * *

"Do you really think the brothers are innocent?" Miles asked Cat.

"Yes."

"Why?"

"I'm not sure. A feeling I have."

"Like when you allowed me to stay at your home? That kind of feeling?"

"Yes. Call it intuition. Also, I doubt they'd be that stupid. They are poor Mexicans, not able to fight against an affluent, well-known artist. A white man. There's no way to prove Beringer raped her. If one of the brothers killed him, or even tried to kill him, it would mean instant jail or even the death penalty. That would create a big hardship for the family as well. The only way I could see one of them killing him would be in a fit of rage. I just think those brothers went with her to support her, and they came away with nothing. They've retreated into their own space now."

Miles nodded. "Makes sense. I've learned again and again how the Anglos have dominated the political and legal systems of the Borderlands. Like us Brits in India and African countries."

"I could be wrong, though. Her brothers are really pissed off. We'll keep them on our list of possible suspects."

They fell silent as Cat drove them back to the east toward Bisbee.

Coming toward them on the narrow highway was a white truck about the size of a UPS delivery truck. Cat paid it little heed until it came much closer. The truck was coming at them really fast, and it seemed to be moving erratically. Just before the truck came even with Cat and Miles, it swerved suddenly from the oncoming lane directly into their path. Cat was forced to veer to her right off the pavement onto the narrow graveled shoulder to avoid a head-on collision. This all happened in seconds.

The sudden jerk of the steering wheel to the right forced their car to go into a skid. It went around in a half a circle then tipped up onto the wheels on the right side of the car. For a heartbeat, the car balanced on two wheels. It was headed toward tipping over and possibly rolling off the highway into the desert sand. Miles shoved his body toward Cat and pushed her toward her door. At the same time, he put his hands between her head and the glass window on her side of the car. The car was on the verge of tipping right so shifting their weight to the left meant that the car bounced down suddenly onto all four wheels to the left. It hit hard, bounced once then came to a stop. Shifting weight meant that the car did not roll out of control but instead, came to a rest in the correct position.

"Miles!" She looked at him, fear in her eyes.

"Are you okay?"

"Yes, thanks to you." She was trembling.

She looked down the highway. The truck had disappeared. "That was on purpose. The guy tried to run us off the road."

Miles nodded. "Did you see his face?"

"Yes. He had on a hoodie and a mask over his face. I saw that just at the last moment before he tried to hit us."

"I also saw that. This was definitely intentional. He wanted us to crash. We could have been seriously injured."

"Thank you for preventing me from hitting my head on the glass."

He nodded.

"You're a fast thinker," she added.

"And you are a good driver. It would have been a lot worse if you had hit the brakes. You managed to control it as well as was possible."

"Luis taught me how to recover from a skid." She took a deep breath. "Let's go home."

"Yes, let's. I could use a cuppa."

Cat started the car again and turned it back to the east. They were silent all the way back to Old Bisbee.

Cat pulled into her driveway at the side of her gallery home. She turned off the engine, but instead of getting out, she said, "Miles, I thank you again for being here for now. I'd be in deep trouble if you weren't. The break-in and now that guy trying to run us off the road make it clear that someone is after me. I don't know why. I need to focus on this problem so I can stay alive."

She wasn't looking at Miles as she spoke. "Also, I want to apologize again for teasing you about your sex life. I know you're British and you are quite reserved, totally unlike this big mouth American you're dealing with. You are a gentleman and not one to brag about sexual exploits. I'm very sorry. I won't do it again." She got out of the car and headed to the back door. She didn't look at him at all.

* * *

Miles sat in silence for a few minutes. The near disaster on the highway was unnerving. She was right. Someone was after her. Why? He was going to have to apply his intellect to the problem, and try to figure out what was going on.

He hated to see Cat so upset. And the phrase she used, 'for now.' They were both acutely aware of the fact that he would be leaving soon.

Also, it was pretty clear to Miles that he'd mishandled her talking to him about sex. She was sharing something intimate. He was grateful that Cat trusted him enough to share, especially about her ex-husband. He also wished with all his heart that he could have been around earlier to rescue her from that obviously mentally ill, obsessive man.

Rescue? Who do you think you are, Miles, Prince Charming? He shook his head. His feelings for Cat were unexpectedly strong. He wanted to hold her. He was so very close to ditching the whole idea of behaving. He wanted to take her into his arms and kiss her with all the passion that she generated in him.

He sighed.

Maybe if he told her about his sex life, she would laugh. That would be good, he thought, if he could make her laugh.

* * *

Miles found Cat in the kitchen making tea.

She looked up at him. "Are you sure you want tea? We could get one of the ales or stouts or whatever."

"Tea is good." He sat down at the table across from her.

Cat stirred her tea. She said nothing. She frowned and stared at her tea cup.

"The first time I had sex, I was sixteen," Miles said.

Cat's eyes went wide. She looked at Miles. Her smile reappeared.

"I was madly in love. I'd tell you her name, but I can't remember it now." He chuckled. "I wanted to marry her and run away to India."

Cat grinned. "India?"

"Yes, India. Having sex felt so good. I couldn't believe that I had waited until I was sixteen to do it for the first time. I kicked myself for not starting earlier." Miles took a sip. "Do you have sugar?"

"No sugar, just agave syrup."

"What's that?"

"It's made from the agave plant. It's sweet. Try it." She reached behind her and retrieved a plastic bottle full of a thick, dark syrup. She handed it to him. "Just a little bit. It's sweeter than sugar. So did you go to India?"

"No. She threw me over for an older boy. He was a star on the rugby team. You know, athletes?" He made a face.

Cat nodded, smiling.

"When I was seventeen, I had two girlfriends. Not at the same time," he said. "Their names were….Katie and….uh…Sarah. Those were more what you might call a 'hook-up.' No plans to run away to India. At the time, I was in sixth form. I had to study for A-levels. I passed my A-levels and then I went off to university. Oxford University to be exact. There were a lot of girls at Oxford."

"Is that right?" she smiled.

"That's enough for now. I'll wait until later to tell you about my university sex life because it was so….," Miles paused and winked at her. "Let's just say that I was quite busy. Or as you put it, I was 'sex positive.'"

Cat nodded her head and chuckled.

"By the way, you were right about the library."

Cat's mouth fell open. "*Really*?"

Miles shrugged and smiled. "Late at night in the book stacks. She was bored. I was bored. So we decided to relieve our boredom."

"And…?" Cat was grinning at him.
"Up against the library wall. Hot and sweet."
"I knew it!"
"Shall we start dinner?" Miles asked.
"As you wish, Sir Miles." Cat laughed.
"Cheeky girl."

9 MARI

The next morning over breakfast, Cat said, "Let's go take a walk and go by the hotel where Freddy Howard is staying. Maybe we can catch him there and find out what he's up to."

Miles nodded. "I like the idea of an early morning walk, too. Perhaps we'll find him in his room before he goes out to breakfast. It's still early."

They quickly took care of the dishes, tidied the kitchen and drank the last of the coffee. They took off walking hand-in-hand down Tombstone Canyon Road to the center of Old Bisbee.

Cat stopped at a steep set of concrete stairs. "Let's go this way." She led Miles up the stairs to a small bed-and-breakfast with a sign out front that said "Hotel Tranquilo." There was a narrow paved road even higher up the hill above the bed-and-breakfast where people came and went or parked their cars.

Cat and Miles went inside and asked for Freddy Howard. The clerk behind the desk rang Howard's room.

"I'm sorry. There's no answer. He must be out. Or never came back."

"What do you mean, never came back?" Cat asked.

"The maid said he hasn't slept in his bed for the past two nights. I mean before last night. I don't know if he was in the room last night or not. He's paid through the end of the week, and his car is still in the parking lot."

Cat thanked the clerk. As she was leaving, she saw a brochure about the upcoming Great Stair Climb. She grabbed it and took it with her.

Outside, Cat looked at Miles and frowned. "I wonder if Howard is out somewhere in a rental truck looking for us so he can drive us off the road again."

"Are you saying you think that was him?"

Cat sighed and shrugged her shoulders. "I have no idea, Miles. That's what's bothering me so much about all this. I just don't understand what's going on. I don't know how to react if I am so completely clueless."

Miles took her hand in his.

Cat took a deep breath. "Meanwhile, Sir Miles, did you know these stairs you just climbed will be part of the race tomorrow?"

"Really? Tomorrow? They're so steep. Are they all like this? And I have to run up them?"

"Only if you want to beat me. Don't worry. I'm going to win."

"Cheeky and arrogant, too," Miles chuckled. "My legs are longer than yours."

"But I know the route. I've done this before."

"Then I'll study the map, and I'll follow you tomorrow. At the last moment, I'll surge ahead and defeat you."

"No way!" Cat poked him in the ribs.

They went back down the staircase. Cat led him around the central canyon so Miles could see other staircases, too.

"Is this race going to kill me?" he grinned.

"Nah. What doesn't kill you makes you stronger."

"Ah, Miss Cheeky Girl is quoting Friedrich Nietzsche."

"Nietzsche? No. It was Pancho Villa who said that!"

Miles threw his head back and roared with laughter. "Good one," he chortled.

Cat was laughing, too. "Oh, look. That's where we'll go for craft beer after the race." She pointed across the street to a large pavilion with tables and chairs set up.

"Or we could just go there first, get drunk and watch everyone running." Miles had a thoughtful look on his face.

"You're such a weenie." She poked him in the ribs again. "Let's go home now. I received a text from Mari Spencer. She's coming this afternoon to fix the hole in the wall."

"What will we do this morning?"

"Let's go in the storeroom off the gallery and do a quick inventory before she arrives."

"Great."

* * *

Back at the gallery, Miles retrieved his laptop and took it downstairs to the storeroom. It had been locked all this time, and now Cat opened it with her key. It was a large room with high windows on two walls. Paintings were stacked along the other walls.

"I was thinking I could make an Excel spreadsheet of everything you document," Miles said.

"Great idea. Let's record the art pieces by title, size, medium, the artist's name, and value, too, if we have that information."

"Will do." Miles set the laptop on a small desk, and plugged it in.

Cat went around the room and looked at each painting. "They are all labeled so it will be easy to put in the spreadsheet."

"Luis was very organized."

"Yes, he was. I learned a lot from him. He told me once that if he hadn't been so interested in art, he would have become a librarian, maybe in an art library or a history library."

"Did Luis have a love interest?"

Cat grew pensive. "He told me that when he was a university student, he fell in love with a girl from Yuma. Her name was Abril. He asked her to marry him, and she said yes. She was from a big Mexican-American family. He said he went out there to Yuma once to visit. The family was very welcoming. One weekend, Abril caught a ride with another student in his car to go visit her family. They were on the highway about an hour east of Yuma when they were hit head-on by a semi. She died instantly. Luis told me this, and then he never talked about it again. He took it pretty hard. He finished his degree and moved back to Bisbee to take care of me. As far as I know, that girl was his only love interest."

"That's sad."

Cat nodded.

For the next hour, Cat systematically went around the room and gave Miles the data on each painting. He entered everything into the spreadsheet.

"What's that big cabinet over there?" Miles asked. He gestured to a large metal cabinet at least six feet wide and nearly that tall with several deep drawers.

"I'm not sure. Let's take a look."

She opened one drawer after another. "It's a collection of folders with different artists' names." She looked into one folder. "Looks like drawings and small paintings on paper. There are also smaller folders with contracts, correspondence, that kind of thing. Come and look."

Miles stood beside Cat. They pulled out one folder labeled with a man's name on it.

"We have one of this guy's paintings in the gallery now," Cat said. "There's a lot of graphite drawings and a couple of soft pastel paintings. Maybe Luis was planning a feature on this artist, or maybe posting his work on our website. Sometimes when people can't afford a large painting, they will buy something smaller instead. Luis made that possible."

"Oh, look!" Miles pointed to a folder labeled "*Mi Hermana.*" That means 'my sister.' Is this your work? Let's take a look."

"Oh, you don't want to look at that," Cat was suddenly very shy.

"Yes, I do! You didn't tell me you're an artist."

"I'm not really. I just play around."

"Let's see." He pulled the folder out and placed it on the table.

"Okay?" He looked at Cat.

"You're going be sorry. But go ahead."

Miles opened the folder. One by one, he looked carefully at the small colorful paintings.

"These are watercolors?"

She nodded. "I mostly do landscapes."

"And you do them very well. These are good."

"Oh, you're just being polite."

He clicked his tongue. "I've studied art, art history to be exact. These are good. I'm not being polite. I'm being truthful." He looked at her and frowned. "You should listen to me sometimes. I occasionally know what I'm talking about. You're quite consistent about refusing to give yourself credit for any number of things. I don't know why. Do you, Cat?"

Cat looked up at him, eyes wide. She didn't know what to say. She shrugged her shoulders.

Miles continued to turn over the drawings one by one to see the next one. Suddenly he came to one that was quite different. It was a landscape. Unlike Cat's paintings with intense desert colors, this one was primarily green. Trees and flowering plants appeared in a hilly landscape with a narrow road running through it. The white of an unpainted sky had loose swaths of pale blue to indicate clouds.

"This doesn't look like your work at all," Miles said. "Yet it looks familiar somehow."

"Oh my god," Cat had her hands covering her cheeks now.

"What is this?" Miles asked.

"Oh, Miles. This is a David Hockney painting. See the initials in the corner."

"Yes, this does look like an English landscape. And that's why it seems familiar."

"He went back to Yorkshire after living for years in California. This was very likely painted there."

"It must be worth quite a few pounds sterling."

"Yes. And even more dollars. But what the hell is it doing here?"

"I think your brother was hiding it."

"I'm beginning to think I didn't know my brother very well at all."

"Here's an envelope with your name on it. It's in among your paintings." Miles handed it to her.

Cat opened it and took out two sheets of paper. The first was a handwritten note from her brother. She read it out loud to Miles.

"Dearest Chiquita."

Cat's eyes filled with tears. "That's what Luis called me in private. *'Chiquita.'*"

She continued to read.

"I'm putting this Hockney watercolor in your folder for safe keeping in case anyone breaks into the gallery and tries to steal anything. This little watercolor is worth more than any other painting in the gallery. I have it as collateral for a loan I made to Jax Beringer. You've met Jax. Turns out that Jax likes to gamble. He recently lost a lot, and he needed some quick cash. So I agreed to loan him ten thousand dollars. He's supposed to pay it back to me in six months, or, failing that, he agreed to give me two of his paintings outright to sell as my own. As I said, this is collateral on the loan. If you stumble upon it, keep it in your folder for safe keeping. Love, Tu Hermano."

Cat put the note back in the envelope. She looked at the second paper. It was a brief note signed by Jax Beringer.

"This David Hockney painting is collateral for a loan I received from Luis Miranda. I will retrieve it upon repayment of the loan."

She looked up at Miles. "Wow."

"You told me that Freddy Howard asked if you had a Hockney," Miles said.

"Yes! I had forgotten about that. He said he 'heard' I had a Hockney. Now how the hell did he know that?'

"If he and Beringer were married, currently or in the past, then maybe that's how he knew about it. In fact, it's possible that the watercolor was joint property from their marriage. Or it may have been Howard's alone, and Beringer just took it when he left California."

"But as far as Howard was concerned, this watercolor could still have been in Beringer's possession," Cat said.

"Maybe Howard found out that Beringer had given it to Luis as collateral on that loan."

"So maybe he was the one who broke into your room that first night so he could look for it."

"When that didn't work, he came here and offered to buy the gallery, figuring if he bought the gallery, he would get everything," Miles added. "The Hockney, Jax's paintings, everything."

"And maybe he's the one who tried to run us off the road to scare me into selling out."

"Very possibly."

"I'm so going to need a lawyer." Cat sighed.

"Yes, you need a lawyer. The Beringer estate owes you ten thousand dollars."

Cat sat down in the nearest chair. "I feel overwhelmed right now."

"Let's take a break now, poppet, and have some lunch."

She looked up at Miles. "What does that word mean?"

"'Poppet'? It's a really old-fashioned word, not used much these days. I use it because I'm an historian, and I like the word. It's a term of affection and admiration. 'Poppet' fits you. I'm feeling a lot of empathy and sympathy for you right now. And affection."

"Thank you, Miles. I appreciate that." She stood up. "Okay, let's make some lunch."

* * *

Mari came as scheduled. She brought her tools in first, then a sheet of dry wall and a bucket with more supplies in it. She put a tarp down on the shining hardwood floor in front of the hole in the wall.

"I precut the dry wall so I wouldn't have to make a lot of noise with an electric saw."

Apparently, Mari had a customer in the past who had complained about noise.

"Okay. Do what you need to do. Miles and I will be in the storage room here. We're doing an inventory of everything."

Cat and Miles started going through some of the folders. It took Mari about two hours to finish the work.

"Cat?" Mari called out. "I'm finished. I could come back and give the wall a second coat of paint. But for now, I think it's okay. You can invite guests in."

"Great. Want to come into the kitchen and have a coffee or tea or a snack? Miles is learning to make Mexican food."

"Sonoran cuisine," he said seriously.

"Are you planning on opening a restaurant in Ireland or England or wherever you came from?"

"I'm English. No, I just want to know how to make this great food because when I go home, I won't be able to find this anywhere, not even in London."

"When I go home…" Cat noticed his words immediately. He was leaving. She was starting to feel a second pain in her heart. *Mierda.* Why do I always do this? she asked herself. Always fall for the wrong guy.

They went into the kitchen, and Cat poured all three a cup of coffee.

"Cat, I want to tell you how much I appreciate your giving me a chance. I love doing this kind of work. I went to Cochise College where I got training and a professional certificate. But too many people think a woman, especially a young one, can't do it. I just need a chance to prove myself."

"You might think about doing some marketing of your services," Cat said. "You'd be surprised to find that there are people willing to give you a chance. Do you have a website or promote yourself on social media?"

"No, I don't know anything about that."

Cat fell silent. Miles reached for his coffee.

"How about this idea?" Cat said. "I worked for a company in Phoenix that did a lot of different services for businesses. I could design a website for you and show you how to keep it updated.

You can draw on the new website material to post on social media. It's extra work, but in the long run, it's worth it for a small business like yours. You'll get new clients."

"That would be great, Cat, but I don't have much money, certainly not enough to pay for a pro like you."

"I have a better idea. I need two things from you. I just found out that I inherited the house next door, and I have this gallery building to take care of, too. I'm sure there will be repairs to be made on both structures. We could have an agreement that you are my go-to carpenter and handyman…or handywoman. You would give me priority over other customers."

Mari grinned. "That would be totally awesome. I agree! What's the second thing?"

"This is more difficult. It looks like I've been targeted for some reason. Someone tried to break in here, I've had two offers to buy me out, and Miles and I nearly got run off the road on purpose yesterday. The worst thing, of course, is that Jax's body was found in *my* wall! I need some help figuring out what is going on. Could you talk a little about Jax, what you know about him, anything that might help me understand all this? I only met him once. I just can't figure out why someone would go to the trouble of stashing his dead body in the wall of our gallery."

Cat glanced at Miles. He was looking at her with a slight smile on his face. He nodded. She could feel his approval at her questions.

"What do you need to know?" Mari was serious now, a sad frown on her face.

"That's just it. I don't know what I need to know. Could you just start talking and I'll ask questions?"

Mari nodded. "I'll try."

"Start with how you met Jax."

"He called me. He said he needed some work done on his wooden porch and railings. I went over and took a look. He hired me on the spot. I went back the next day, replaced the railings and a couple of planks on the porch. When I finished, he asked me to stay for dinner."

"So one thing led to another?" Cat asked.

"Yeah, I had broken up from my long-time boyfriend about six months ago. I was missing male companionship…if you know what I mean." Mari looked at Miles and smiled. He looked down at his coffee cup.

"Jax was very charming and funny at first. He was very attentive to me and made me feel special. I continued to go to his place at his invitation for dinner and conversation. We started kissing a lot. Then he asked me to model for him."

"I didn't know he did figurative work," Cat said.

"You mean naked pictures?" Mari asked.

"Well, by 'figurative,' I mean any paintings or drawings of people, not necessarily nude."

"Jax wanted nude. I agreed. I had already decided to sleep with him if he asked. I felt like I was falling in love with him. And he did ask me to sleep with him, right after the first nude modeling session." Mari shook her head. "I was an idiot. I thought he had feelings for me, too."

"So this went on for a while?"

"Yes, about a month. Then one day he was really cold to me when I arrived at his house. He told me he was ending our relationship. He said he was bored and tired of me. He didn't have to say such cruel things, but he did. He laughed at me when I began to cry."

Cat glanced at Miles. He was staring at his coffee cup and frowning.

"So what happened?"

"I got really mad. I mean I've been putting up with a lot of crap from people, and then this guy that I had fallen for treated me like shit. I cried, but I also started yelling at him. My tool box was there in his living room. I reached down and picked up my dad's hammer and I threw it at him. I was furious."

"Did you hit him?"

"No. He caught the hammer by the handle. Like a baseball player or something. He laughed. Then he told me to get out."

"What happened to the hammer?" Miles asked. It was the first time he'd spoken.

"The bastard kept it. It was my daddy's hammer. My dad died when I was sixteen. He showed me how to use the tools, and when he died, the tools came to me. That hammer had special meaning to me. And Jax refused to return it."

"You asked him for it again?" Cat asked.

"Yes. He said no, and told me to get off his property. I thought about breaking in when he wasn't there to get my hammer, but I decided not to do that. If I got caught, he's just the kind of shit who would file charges against me. I don't need to go to jail."

"Could you describe the hammer? Any unique characteristics?" Miles ask.

"The handle was wooden and pretty old, too. I oiled it to keep it in good condition. The hammer head had a little notch in it. I had to be careful how to use it so I wouldn't put notches in anything that I hammered."

Cat glanced at Miles. He nodded his head. She turned again to Mari. "Now that Jax is dead, you may be able to get it back," Cat said.

"That would great," Mari said. She paused. "You know that big painting you have in your gallery, the one with the lips?"

"Yes, it's titled 'Kissed,'" Cat said.

"I hate that painting. Jax said he did it for me. He said I should feel grateful that he would make a painting for me. Arrogant shit."

Cat shook her head. She glanced at Miles. He was frowning again.

"I guess that's all I have to tell you. I had a brief affair with a guy who was charming, and then he turned into a total asshole. And he stole my favorite tool."

She fell silent. Then Mari's face changed from brooding to something different. Cat noticed this immediately.

Mari's gaze had shifted toward Miles, and now she was smiling. She turned to Cat and said, "*Es muy guapo. ¿Es tu novio?*" He's very handsome. Is he your boyfriend?"

Cat glanced at Miles. He was biting his lower lip. He had turned a slight shade of pink.

"No," Cat answered. "*Regresa a Inglaterra muy pronto.*" He's returning to England very soon.

"*Quizás puedas seducirlo antes de que se vaya.*" Perhaps you can seduce him before he goes. Mari giggled and winked at Cat.

Cat heard an odd noise and looked at Miles.

His face was red, and his eyes were wide open. He shoved his hand over his mouth, turned to his left, and spewed out a mouthful of coffee onto the floor. He began coughing violently, bending over at the waist.

Cat stood up and patted him on the back. "Are you okay?"

"Yes," Miles managed to wheeze. He finally got control and said, "Sorry. Sorry. I choked." Then he coughed some more. He was red in the face, and he had tears in his eyes. "I'll clean this up." He reached for paper towels and bent down to wipe up the coffee. He coughed again.

Mari rose and said, "Guess I better go. That's all I have to tell you."

"That helps. Thanks so much."

"I'll send you an email invoice. Call me when you need me again."

"Okay. And you send me some photos of yourself and completed projects. Even better would be some before-and-after photos of completed projects. As soon as we resolve this trouble I'm in, I'll start designing a website for you."

Mari said her goodbyes to both of them.

Miles had control of his breathing again. Only an occasional cough came out.

"I guess she didn't know that I can understand Spanish," he said.

"I guess not," Cat chuckled.

"This was informative. I'm learning a lot about American women."

Cat grinned and laughed. "So, Sir Miles, what did you learn today?"

"You American women are...," he hesitated. "You're not shy about saying what you want."

She nodded. "Some of us, anyway." Am I being shy? she asked herself.

Then Miles became quiet. He looked at Cat directly in the eyes. He was serious now. "I promised to behave. But you didn't, Cat. You don't have to behave. Not at all."

Cat felt herself growing warm. She looked down, avoiding eye contact. She knew what he was saying, and she didn't know how to respond. Best to change the subject.

"It appears that Jax may have been killed by Mari's hammer," she said finally, her voice a little shaky.

"Yes, the autopsy will no doubt confirm that."

"So I'm guessing someone wants to pin this on Mari...."

"Or Jax was beaten in a fit of rage by some other person," Miles added.

"Apparently he enraged a lot of people," Cat said.

"Yeah, he was a real wanker."

Cat sighed. "It's getting late," she said. "Time to start dinner."

"Very well, m'lady. I'll help you."

* * *

That evening, Cat and Miles took a walk again. They went past the B&B where Howard was staying, but he was not there. They went up Brewery Gulch, stopped off at Amanda's tavern for a pint, and sat together listening to music and conversation in the crowded bar. Then they wound their way through Bisbee's streets back home again.

"Tomorrow is the Great Stair Climb, Miles," Cat said. "I'm going to bed early so I'll be rested and ready. I'm going to beat your pants off."

Miles made a funny face and laughed.

Cat blushed. "Never mind! Good night, Sir Miles." She went into her room, closed the door, came out a few minutes later in that gown he so admired, went to the bathroom, then back to her room. She left her bedroom door partly open.

Cat put her head on her pillow and stared at the ceiling. She was thinking about Miles. She wanted to go to him, but she didn't. Finally, she fell asleep.

Miles went to his room, opened his laptop and turned it on, and began an email letter to his dad. He explained what was going on there, the body in the wall, the investigation, and his concern for Cat's safely.

In his final paragraph, Miles said, "*To top it all off, I have growing feelings for this young woman. She's lovely, sweet, and funny. It's going to be really hard for me to leave her. But I have to leave. I signed a contract with the uni in Exeter. I start teaching classes about ten days after I return home. I can't break the contract or I'll never get another one. So it's really important to me that Cat is safe before I go. I just wish I could bring her home with me. Love, Miles*"

He looked at the email. Then he deleted the last line about taking Cat with him back to England. She would never leave here. She was part of the Borderlands. She would be totally out of place and miserable in England. She didn't even like Phoenix. This was her home and Miles would have to leave her here. He felt a real sadness to even think of leaving Catalina Amalia Miranda. But what choice did he have?

10 The Race

"Today is the day of the big race," Cat grinned. She was standing at his bedroom door, her head inserted into Miles's bedroom. "I'll go make coffee."

"Oh my god, it's still dark outside," Miles groaned.

"We have to be there early to get our bib numbers. We can eat breakfast at the parish hall and watch the parade, too. We have to be ready to run at our corrals at 7:55 am. So get up, get up, get up!"

He groaned again.

Cat was already heading down the stairs to the kitchen. She could hear Miles upstairs hauling himself out of bed. He showed up in the kitchen not long after, dressed in a long-sleeved cotton t-shirt and some loose fleece pants, similar to Cat's outfit. She also noticed that he had gone without shaving.

"So tell me about this, Cat. What should I expect?"

"There's going to be a lot of people. Hundreds. But they limit participants to one thousand five hundred. People come from out of town to participate. There are all age groups, too. The starts are staggered, and they will time us to see who wins in our group."

Cat was excited and happy. She had participated in several of Bisbee's Great Stair Climbs. For a while anyway, she could put out of her mind the body in the wall of her gallery, the murder which most certainly had occurred, the intruder who tried to break into her house, and the man in the truck who tried to drive her off the road. She could be herself for a little while and have some fun. Have some fun with Miles.

"Fifteen hundred people. That's a lot," Miles said.

"Can be, especially if you are all trying to get up a set of stairs at the same time. There are prizes and an awards ceremony, too," she added.

"I'll be happy if you just beat my pants off. That's what you said yesterday." He grinned at her.

"That's just an idiom. You can keep your pants on."

"So how long is this race?"

"Four point five miles."

"That's all?"

"Yes, but you have to run up nine staircases and over one thousand steps. Also some of the roads we will be running on will gain elevation, too. So it's not easy."

"Are you sure you don't want to just go to that pavilion and drink beer?"

"No. I want to race."

"Competitive, are we?"

"I'm going to beat you."

"Beat my pants off? I'm going to hold you to that."

"Miles, be good. Stop flirting with me." Cat returned his smile. "Although I bet you have nice legs."

"Oh, I do. Want to see them?"

"No! I want to be on time for the race."

"Okay. Then I'll show you my legs later. May I see your legs, too?"

Cat rolled her eyes. "Just finish your coffee!"

Miles drained his cup.

"Okay. Ready."

Cat and Miles took off walking down Tombstone Canyon at a quick pace. Cat took his hand in hers and pulled Miles when he lagged. She noticed that he, too, seemed especially pleased with the world this morning.

As they came closer to the center of town, they were joined by more and more people ready for the run. Cat pulled Miles across a parking lot to a church, St. Patrick's.

"We can get breakfast here," she said.

"I think I'd better not eat much," Miles said, "I don't want to lose this race."

Cat looked at him like he was crazy. "You *are* going to lose. You don't have a chance against me."

"Actually there's no way I can lose. Either I'll win the race out-right, or I'll lose and lose my pants in the process. Actually I'm quite looking forward to losing my pants. If that's losing, then I win."

Cat laughed and shook her head.

They entered the parish hall to find racers at long tables eating breakfast. Cat and Miles both retrieved small plates of scrambled eggs, a biscuit, some fruit, and more coffee.

After breakfast, they went out to join fellow racers. They collected their bib numbers and pinned them to their shirts. Someone handed them a map of the race. Along the way, Cat ran into several people she knew. She traded hugs and a few words with them all. She introduced Miles to everyone.

They wandered around for a while, then Cat said, "Okay! It's time to go to our corrals. The race is about to start."

Cat was bouncing up and down on her toes and grinning. Miles began to laugh.

"Why are you laughing?" she asked.

"Why are you jumping up and down?" he countered.

"I'm excited."

"I'm excited, too. I'm about to lose my pants to a beautiful girl."

"Shut up!" Cat smiled. "You have a one-track mind."

"What do we do now?"

"The gun will go off and the first group will take off," Cat explained to Miles. "Then it will be our turn because we're in the next group."

Miles was looking at the map.

"We'll run along Main Street, go up Brewery Avenue, then we'll see the first set of stairs," Cat pointed to the map. "Seventy-three stairs."

Miles made a face. "Seventy-three! Sure you're not trying to kill me?"

"No, I only want your pants," Cat giggled. She was feeling so good that she figured she'd just play along and deal with the consequences later.

Miles's eyebrows went up, and he laughed, "That's my girl."

"Actually seventy-three is the one with the least number of stairs. The one with the most has one hundred eighty-one."

Now it was his turn to shake his head in dismay.

The gun went off, and the first wave of runners took off running. Cat was jumping up and down again, and Miles was laughing again.

"Ready? Here we go," Cat said. Their wave was released, and off they went.

The run down Main Street was easy, and the first set of seventy-three stairs not bad at all. Then the race became more and more challenging as the staircases grew longer, with more and more steps.

Cat looked back at Miles. His face was pink and his strawberry blond hair was ruffled and unkempt as always. He was grinning at her. She figured her face was probably pink, too. She hadn't felt this happy in months, or maybe even years. She looked up at the sky so blue and down at her feet. In this moment, running with her handsome Englishman, life was good.

Next came one hundred stairs, then one hundred eighty-one, seventy-eight, one hundred fifty-one. After that came a long run back to the west along High Road, Tombstone Canyon Road, Garden Avenue, then another set of one hundred thirty steps.

Cat knew that this was the sixth set of stairs out of a total of nine. She and Miles were not too far from her home. She wondered if he would bail out on her now or continue running. Much to her surprise, he surged past her on the sixth set of stairs. He patted her on her bottom as he passed her. She could hear him laughing as he went past.

* * *

Miles was running rapidly, taking the steps two at a time. Cat could see that he was very close to the top.

All that about losing his pants, but the truth is that he just can't stand letting me win, she laughed to herself. Now who's the competitive one? Oh, she was going to tease him to no end.

Suddenly and without warning, a man jumped out from behind a tree only a few feet from the staircase. He was dressed in a black hoodie pulled up to cover his head, and he had a blue paper mask over his lower face. He slammed violently into Cat and shoved her off the stairs and onto the rocky ground.

The man's body knocking into hers hurt her in the rib cage. But at the same time, Cat felt her left foot go off the edge of the concrete steps at an awkward angle. She yelped in pain when she hit the ground. The wind was knocked out of her for a couple of seconds by the violent jolt. Worse, the man allowed himself to fall on top of her. He lay there for a few seconds, his upper arms jammed against her chest just below her throat. Then he jumped up, ran away on the steps in a downhill direction. He disappeared into a small grove of trees. Cat struggled against the terror she felt. She was vaguely aware that Miles had yelled out her name. She glanced up and saw him at the top of the stairs. He had already started down the stairs toward her, running in a rapid dash. He knelt at her side.

"I saw that bloke. He hit you. Are you hurt? I heard you cry out."

"I think I landed on a rock. My back hurts. And my chest where he hit me. I'll probably have a bruise." She tried to stand up. When she put her weight on her ankle, she nearly fell. Miles caught her.

"I think maybe I sprained my ankle."

Miles was still holding her up. Cat looked up at him. He was looking down the hillside where the attacker had disappeared.

"That bastard," he growled. "Do you know him?"

"No. I don't think so. He had on a mask so I couldn't see his face." She groaned.

"I can't go after him now. I can't leave you. I think you're going to need some help."

Cat looked at his face. Miles looked very distressed. And angry.

"I'm okay." Cat took a step forward. She couldn't help herself. She cried out in pain and would have collapsed, but Miles caught her again.

"I'm going to carry you home," he said firmly.

"No. I can do it."

Again, Cat made a feeble attempt to walk. She whimpered as her weight fell on the ankle.

"What do you mean 'no'? I said I'm carrying you home. You can't walk on that ankle."

"I'm too big for you to carry me."

"You are not too big. How tall are you?"

"Five feet one."

"Oh my god. That's *so* big," Miles said in an annoyed voice. "I bet you only weigh eight or nine stone."

"Stone? I'm big!"

"No, you're not. You have big breasts, but you're not big."

"I can't believe you said that." She felt heat flood through her body.

"I'm a bloke. Blokes notice these things." He moved toward her. "Here, I'm going to carry you home."

Cat frowned. Her mouth was in a tight line. Tears appeared in her eyes.

"*No.* I'm too heavy."

Miles stood up straight. Now he was the one who frowning. "You're so spoiled. Such a little princess. You can't have your own way all the time, and you're not getting it now. Don't argue with me. I'm already cheesed off."

Cat spit out, "Be cheesed off, whatever that means. I don't need you to carry me. And I'm *not* a princess." Suddenly her anger disappeared. Tears spilled out of her eyes, and rolled down her cheeks. She struggled to control a sob.

"Bugger it all," Miles said in an exasperated voice. "Don't cry. I don't know what to do when you cry."

Cat looked up at him. "I can't help it. I'm hurting." Tears continued to roll down her cheeks.

"Will you *please* let me help you?" Miles frowned. His jaw jutted out. "Never mind. I'm taking over now, and I'm helping you, whether you like it or not."

Before she could say anything, he stepped forward, leaned down and scooped her up in his arms.

"Put your arms around my neck. Cooperate with me. And don't talk," he commanded.

"Okay," she whispered. She didn't know what to think. She'd never seen Miles be even the slightest bit annoyed.

"We just go along here on this road to the west, correct?"

"That's right. I'll tell you when to turn off and head downhill."

"Good."

Miles walked steadily and carefully.

As for Cat, she did as he insisted. She put her arms around his neck and shoulders. Then she pulled herself closer to him. She snuggled her face against his jaw and neck.

"That's better," he said. "I'm going to walk slowly so I don't trip on a rock. I want to get you home and put some ice on that ankle."

Cat cuddled against him. She felt safe. Miles smelled good in a man kind of way. She suppressed a strong urge to kiss his neck and ears. He hadn't shaved so he had stubble on his face. She decided that the stubble was sexy. Clean-shaven was sexy, too. Probably a beard would be sexy. Miles was sexy.

After a few minutes of silent walking on the trail, Miles said, "I apologize for calling you a princess. You're actually quite brave. Will you forgive me?"

Cat said, "Yes, I forgive you." She paused. "You're right. I can be a handful sometimes."

That made Miles chuckle. "Indeed, m'lady. Indeed."

She snuggled closer.

Miles smiled. "I like what you are doing now."

"What's that?"

"Being quiet and cuddling up to me. Let's do this more often. Not the hurt. I mean the cuddling."

"You're sweet," Cat whispered.

They came to a place along the trail, and Cat pointed to a narrower trail. "Go down that way, and we'll be only a block from my place."

Miles did as she said. In a short time, they were at Cat's back door. Miles put her down. "Lean against me." He found the key in his pocket and opened the back door. He carried her into the house, and kicked the door shut behind him.

"You can't carry me up the stairs," she frowned.

"Remember that part about being quiet and cooperating with me?"

"Okay. Okay. Okay."

Up the stairs they went, Miles carrying Cat. He took her to her room and placed her on her bed. He stuffed a pillow under her injured ankle.

"I'll be back in a minute with some ice." Miles went down the stairs again.

Cat could hear him in the kitchen. He returned with a glass of water and some aspirin as well as a plastic bag filled with ice.

"Take the aspirin, and I'll get a towel. Do you happen to have an elastic bandage?"

"Look in the box in the bathroom cabinet. I think there's one there."

Miles went to the bathroom and returned with a towel and an elastic bandage. In short order, he had the towel-wrapped ice pack placed firmly under and around her ankle.

Cat laid back, her head on the pillow. After taking care of her dying brother for two months, it was strange to have someone caring for her. Strange and also very comforting. Miles was very business-like about the whole process.

"Now," he said, "we'll make sure your ankle isn't going to swell too much. Then we'll put on this elastic bandage. That will help with swelling, too. We'll just have to make sure it's not too tight because we don't want to hamper circulation."

Miles sat down on the bed next to her stretched-out body.

"You seem to know a lot about this," Cat said.

"I have lots of experience with sprains and muscle strains and the like. My mates and I took care of each other unless the injury was bad. Then we called the team doctor."

"The team doctor? What team?"

"I was on the track and field team in secondary school, upper and lower sixth form, and university, too."

She gasped. "Oh, *you*. You didn't tell me you're a runner. And on the track team no less. Sprinter or long distance?"

"Both. I'm fast, but I prefer long distance. I run marathons."

"You could have beaten me in a nanosecond."

"But that would have taken all the fun out of it," he smiled. "I've never had a *chica bonita* beat the pants off of me."

"*Chica bonita*? I'm not a pretty girl. I'm just an ordinary Mexican-American girl."

Miles shook his head. "I have no idea why you think that. Have you looked in the mirror lately? You are most definitely a pretty girl." He took her hand in his. "Hush now, you need some kip. Close your eyes and rest a bit."

"What's 'kip'?"

"A little siesta."

Cat closed her eyes. Then she sat up suddenly, wrapped her arms tightly around herself and leaned forward. She leaned her head against Miles's chest.

Miles put his arms around her and held her close.

"Did you hear what he said?" Cat muttered.

"The man who attacked you? No. What did he say?"

"He told me to get out of town or he would kill me."

Miles pulled her even closer and held her.

"I'm scared," Cat whispered.

Miles nodded. He held her for long minutes until he felt her relax and sag against him. Her breathing turned from ragged to rhythmic and soft. He leaned forward, cradling her in his arms until she was resting on her pillow again. Cat had drifted off to sleep. Miles waited, holding her hand, until he was sure she was well asleep. He bent and kissed her on her forehead and then left her to her nap.

* * *

Miles went downstairs and called the Bisbee Police Department. He spoke in a quiet voice so that he wouldn't wake Cat. His conversation with Sam Morales was brief. He summed up by saying, "I couldn't follow the attacker and take him down because Cat was hurt and needed my help getting home. She sprained her ankle, bruised her back and was scared. Too bad I couldn't chase him because it would have been pretty easy to catch him and put a stop to all this. Now the wanker has threatened her. When can you get here?" There was a pause. "All right, then. See you this afternoon."

He sat at the kitchen table and worried. This situation had become much more serious now. The stranger's intrusion was an unpleasant event, but that could just have been someone attempting to execute a robbery. The body in the wall was bad, clearly a case of murder. However, that discovery didn't seem to have anything to do with Cat directly. The attempt to run them off the road seemed like an aggression. But now this. A direct death threat against her. This wouldn't do.

Miles clenched his fists. He wasn't going to allow anyone to hurt Cat. He had to find out who was behind this and why. He decided to call his dad and ask for help. Miles went back upstairs and sat in his room staring at the pages of a book. His intention was to read until Cat woke up, but he couldn't concentrate. He couldn't think about anything but Cat. Finally, he heard her stirring. He went to her.

11 Advice

Cat sat up in bed. She looked up. Miles was at her door.

"Feeling better, m'lady?"

"I'm not hurting so much. Thank you, Miles, for taking care of me."

He came to her side and removed the bag of ice. "Your ankle looks good. Let's try putting the elastic bandage on."

"Then I can walk?"

Miles frowned. "Not sure about that. Let's wait a bit."

"I have a cane. Actually it was Luis's cane. It's over there in the corner."

Miles looked and saw a wooden walking cane leaning against the wall. "Good. That will take some weight off your ankle when you try to walk again."

Cat smiled at him. "You'd make a good doctor." She couldn't remember having anyone take such good care of her, not since Luis was there.

"I *am* a doctor," he smiled.

"I mean a medical doctor, not a history doctor."

"Are you hungry? I'll make you some lunch."

"Sure. Maybe I am a princess after all. You're treating me like one."

Miles nodded. "Oh, by the way, I called your police officer, Officer Morales. He's coming by this afternoon. So how about some hot soup? Does that sound good?"

"That sounds great. Should I go downstairs?"

"No, I'll bring it up."

He returned ten minutes later with two bowls of soup, spoons, and crackers on a tray. They ate together in silence. Miles took their dishes back downstairs when they'd finished. When he returned, he took a look again at her ankle.

"Looks good, m'lady. Almost no swelling. It is bruised, though. How about your back where you fell on the rock?"

She turned away from him, and he lifted her t-shirt.

He bent down and looked. "Yes, I see a bruise there, too." He touched her back where there was a big, ugly blue bruise. He stroked the skin softly.

Cat shivered. "Oh, that tickles, but it feels good, too, when you touch me."

He chuckled. "Yes, touching you feels really good, for me I mean."

"Thank you, Miles."

"Oh yes, when I was downstairs, I received a call from Morales. He may be a bit late. He's dealing with a bunch of Great Stair Climb party boys and girls who drank a bit too much."

Cat nodded. "That's part of this event for some folks."

"I'm going to go call my dad now before it gets too late. He's seven hours ahead of us so it's nearly eight in the evening where he is."

"Why are you calling your dad? Is he okay?"

"Yes, he's doing well. I want to call him to get his ideas about this situation we find ourselves in. He was a copper."

"A copper? Your dad was a policeman?"

"Yes, he started as a copper on the street and worked his way up to detective and eventually to superintendent before he retired early so he could take of Mum. I'll come and get you as soon as I get him on Skype."

Miles disappeared into his room. Within five minutes, Cat could hear him talking to his dad. She could even hear his dad's voice. What was his name? Oh, yes. Ian Trevelyan. He and Miles sounded a lot alike to her.

Miles appeared at her door. "Ready?" Before Cat could answer, he came to her bedside and picked her up again. He took her to his room and sat her in a chair next to his at the desk. The laptop was open, and Cat could see Ian Trevelyan smiling at her. He and Miles looked very much alike despite a thirty-year difference. The strawberry blond hair turned a bit white over time.

"Hello, Cat. I'm so pleased to meet you," Ian Trevelyan said.

Cat smiled, "Pleased to meet you, too. Your son insists on carrying me everywhere."

"I would, too, if I were him. You are a very pretty young woman."

"No, I'm not really," she looked down, very embarrassed. "You and Miles think that just because I'm not what you're accustomed to. I'm an ordinary Mexican-American girl. I'm not an English rose."

"You are much prettier than anyone in my neighborhood. Folks from around here are rather plain."

Cat blurted out before even thinking, "You're kidding. Your son's from there. Look at him. He's gorgeous." She realized what she'd just said. Her hand came up and covered her mouth. Miles and Ian were both laughing now.

"And you haven't even seen my legs," Miles said.

Ian nodded. "Well, you could show her your legs."

"Oh, I hope to do just that."

Cat shook her head. "I talk too much. And Mr. Trevelyan, you are as ornery your son." She frowned and looked at him sternly.

Father and son laughed again.

Ian Trevelyan said, "So let's get started. Give me the details of the case."

Miles started. He told his dad about the intruder that tried to break in on Miles's first night in Bisbee, about the dead body found in the wall, about the attempt to run them off the highway, and about the man who had attacked Cat just a few hours earlier.

Cat added details about the body in the wall, his identity, the carpenter Mari who may have been the owner of the murder weapon, about the sudden offers to buy her out, and about the David Hockney watercolor she and Miles had found unexpectedly.

"Really? An authentic David Hockney?" Ian asked.

"Yes, it's even signed by the artist."

"That's worth a few quid, I'd venture to say. Do you have post-mortem results yet?"

"No," Miles said. "We expect those soon. But it seems pretty clear that this bloke was beaten to death by that hammer with the notch in its head."

Ian Trevelyan was quiet for a minute or two.

"First, it seems that you are most certainly in danger, Cat. I suggest that Miles stay by your side until this is resolved. Then you can hire a bodyguard, or if need be, leave your little town and find a safe place to hide until this is over. That latter suggestion is preferable. My experience with these small towns is that the police force is often overwhelmed and not able to adequately protect you."

"Right. There's only one police officer in Bisbee. This isn't a very big town," Miles said.

"We have the sheriff and his deputies," Cat added.

"But they have to cover the entire county," Miles countered. "Cochise County is quite large, over six thousand square miles."

Ian nodded. "Large, indeed. Sussex is seven hundred sixty nine square miles, roughly one tenth the size of Cochise County. I think it unlikely that you can count on round-the-clock protection. By the way, what does that word 'Cochise' mean?"

"Cochise was a Native American. He was an Apache warrior and a chief," Miles said.

Ian shook his head and smiled. "Miles, my boy, I think you have dropped yourself down into a Western."

Miles nodded. "It's quite nice here….except for this bloke who is after Cat."

Ian continued, "So we can conclude that there really aren't enough police officers or sheriff's deputies to watch you twenty-four hours a day, Cat. Miles is just one man. He won't be there forever. Leaving Bisbee may be your safest option."

"But that's what that guy wants. He wants to drive me away." Her frustration was apparent.

"It appears to me that the culprit wants something, we don't know what, and you're in the way, Cat. Obviously, the Hockney watercolor has a lot of value. But you wouldn't have to be eliminated for someone to get it. There are ways to acquire art other than killing the gallery owner. That fellow who wants to buy the gallery, Mr. Howard? You say he and the artist were legally married? Perhaps he thought he could make a claim on it as marital property. Or he may have discovered that wasn't possible so he decided to just buy out the gallery and everything in it. If he has a lot of money, that would be the easiest route. Perhaps he has an emotional attachment to the Hockney as well as a financial interest. That brings up the issue of the artist's estate, and the probate process. Does America have probate courts?"

"Yes," Cat and Miles said together.

"But why someone would hide a dead body in the gallery wall is quite intriguing. It's possible that the murderer thought he could get away with hiding the body, and no one would know for sure that the dead artist was really dead. That brings up the manner of death. If no one knows that the artist is dead, then there would no indication of how he was killed. Perhaps the killer thinks the murder weapon will be linked back to him…or to her. If the body had never been discovered, then no one would know that the artist was dead, or how he died. And there would be no suspicion cast on the murderer."

"So what do you think we should do, Dad?"

"It appears to me that there are two people you must talk to. The first is the man who asked for the Hockney. Find him and learn how he knew about it and why he wants it. His claim could easily be managed in the probate process. For now, I wouldn't tell him that you have the Hockney artwork. It's more important to learn his motivations so you can know how best to handle him. But I don't mean for *you* to handle him. Your solicitor should do that."

"We've been looking for Freddy Howard," Cat said.

"However, I think the second person is the actual murderer. I think he is most likely the one who attacked you, Cat. Other than avoiding a situation where suspicion is cast on him for the death of the artist, I suspect that there is something else going on."

"Like what, Dad?"

"Perhaps a crime of passion. The murderer killed the artist as an act of hatred. It could have been a calculated murder or done in a sudden act of rage. You won't know until you discover who he or she is and why he or she was so furiously angry toward the deceased. That's where I would start, Miles. Try to find out who hated the artist and wanted him dead."

Cat shook her head. "Apparently, a lot of people hated Jax Beringer. What do you think about the brothers of the young girl who was raped by the artist?"

"Possible, but unlikely. Her brothers would have no reason to stash the body in the gallery wall. If one or both of them were the killers, they likely would have left his body where they killed him or dumped it somewhere. That brings up another issue. The murderer wanted the artist dead and his body hidden. But the body need not be hidden in the gallery wall. That suggests a kind of message the murderer was sending to the dead artist and perhaps to the world. Yes, many people hated the artist. But only one was willing to kill him. Only one hated him so much that he hid the artist's body in the wall behind his painting. The painting itself may have a role in this crime of passion. The bottom line is that only one person wanted the artist to know that he, the murderer, had won the struggle between them. There's a kind of defiant exultation in this murder. That is the person you must find."

"You're confirming what Cat and I have speculated. We agree that there was something very personal about killing the artist and then disposing of his body in the wall of the gallery behind the artist's painting."

Ian Trevelyan nodded. "My last word to you, son, and to you, Cat, is to be very careful. You're dealing with a ruthless killer."

Cat sighed.

"Tired, m'lady? I'll take you back to bed. Back in a minute, Dad." Miles rose and picked up Cat. He returned her to her room.

"Let's keep your ankle elevated for a while longer. You rest. I'm going to say goodbye to my dad."

Miles returned to his bedroom. He closed the door quietly behind him. He didn't want Cat to hear him.

"Dad, I'm very concerned about this turn of events. I'm less concerned now about the intruder who tried to break in my first night here. But to have someone try to run Cat off the road and then attack and threaten her. It's too much. I believe she's in serious danger."

Ian Trevelyan nodded. "Do you think you can convince her to leave for a while?"

Miles shook his head. "I don't know. I doubt it. She's very attached to being here. She can be a bit stubborn, too."

"She's very pretty, and she seems sweet, too."

Miles nodded. "I have feelings for her."

"I can see that," Ian said seriously. "It's all over your face and in your voice."

"You know me too well, Dad."

"You can try to get her out of there. Ask her if she wants to have a vacation in England. She could come back here with you."

Miles frowned. "There's no guarantee that local law enforcement would be able to find the killer while she was gone. When she came back here, she'd be in danger again. Also I think she'd probably last about five minutes in rainy, cloudy England. She's what they call a 'desert rat' here."

Ian smiled, "Describe England as green and pleasant land."

Miles returned his smile. "Yes, but it's not the Borderlands. She belongs here."

They both fell silent.

"I'm going to do my best to find out who is behind all this."

Ian nodded. "Watch your back, son."

They signed off. Miles opened his door. He peeked into Cat's room. She was on her bed staring at the ceiling.

"Everything okay?"

"Miles, come and sit with me." She patted a space on the bed beside her.

He sat next to her and took her hand in his.

"I've been thinking," she said.

Miles nodded.

"If you loved someone and the one you loved disappeared, you would try to find that person, right? And if that person turned up dead, you'd probably want to be near them or be near their stuff, right? Maybe get a keepsake for yourself?"

"Ah. You're thinking of Freddy Howard?"

"Yes. I think it's likely that Howard has heard about Beringer's death. You know how Bisbee gossip gets around. Everybody knows everything within forty-eight hours, usually faster. Howard hasn't been at his B&B for a couple of days. I bet we'll find him at Beringer's house."

"That makes a lot of sense."

"We could go there right away, but this ankle is holding me up."

"Let's wait until tomorrow morning. I'm fairly certain that you'll be able to walk a bit, especially if you use the cane. I'll help you. And if it gets to be too much, I'll carry you."

Cat smiled. "I promise I'll cooperate."

"Good."

"One other thing. I ran this morning, and I got all sweaty. I'd really like to have a shower. Will you help me?

Miles swallowed hard.

Cat looked at him. His face had turned pink.

"I just meant that I need help to get this bandage off my leg, to get into the bathroom, and all that. I can undress and dress myself."

"I think it best you have a bath, not a shower, so you can be off your feet. Of course I'll help you. Sure you don't want me to undress you?" he smiled and wiggled his eyebrows.

Cat returned his smile. "I'll manage. Thank you, Miles."

* * *

They heard a knock on the door downstairs. Police officer Sam Morales was at the back door.

"Sorry I'm so late," Sam apologized. "Most of the participants in the Great Stair Climb are great. Totally well-behaved. But there are always a few who like to get drunk after the race."

"Come on up, Officer Morales. Cat is on her bed with her ankle propped up. You can sit on her little settee couch. She's willing to answer your questions."

They went up the stairs, and Miles led Sam Morales into Cat's room. She was sitting up on her bed. She smiled when she saw Sam.

Cat and Sam exchanged greetings. Sam Morales sat down on her settee and pulled out his notebook.

"Okay. Tell me everything. Go slow if you need to. Details matter."

Cat recounted everything she could remember. Then Miles chipped in with what he had noticed.

Sam asked a few questions. He closed his notebook.

"Have you considered leaving for a while, Cat?"

"Oh, I guess if I have no other choice, I will. But Miles will be here a little while longer. I feel safe with him."

Sam Morales nodded. "Oh, by the way, I have results from Beringer's autopsy."

"Really?" Cat said. "Can you share? Maybe we'll notice something that will help your investigation."

"I can't give you a copy of the report, but I can tell you about it. First, the body is definitely Jax Beringer's. We have a firm identification. Second, the cause of death was blunt force trauma. He was beaten to death."

"And the instrument used to kill him?" Miles asked.

"We think it was a hammer like a carpenter uses. The round-shaped wounds are the same size as a standard hammer head. The ME said the wounds are consistent in indicating only one weapon was used. We don't know for sure until we find it, but she told us to look first for a hammer."

"We're not surprised to hear this, Sam. This is what Miles and Eric and I all thought – a hammer. And one with a head that has some kind of notch in it."

"That's correct," Sam said. "No way to know what caused the notch, but it's pretty clear that if and when we find the right hammer, it will be easy to identify as the murder weapon."

He paused and frowned.

"There's one other thing."

Cat and Miles look at him expectantly.

"Beringer was eviscerated."

"Ewww," Cat said in disgust. "You mean his guts were taken it? Oh, gross."

"More than just his intestines, Cat. Someone had taken a knife and cut Beringer from stem to stern starting at his neck and going all the way down to his lower abdomen. He was disemboweled. Everything came out: intestines, stomach, all the organs like kidneys, heart, lungs, liver, you name it." Sam Morales looked almost as distressed as Cat to have to describe the process.

"That explains why there was no smell and why the body was mummifying," Miles said thoughtfully.

"Right," Sam said. "Smell from a decaying body starts when the guts and all the inside stuff starts to bloat and stink. Without all those parts still in the body and with the dry air and lack of exposure to moisture, the rest of the body began to turn into a mummy."

"But wouldn't there be a lot of blood and stuff left?" Cat asked.

"Yes, the hammer blows alone would no doubt leave some evidence because the blows would likely cause blood sprays. We're going to be looking for that. But as far as the evisceration, if this occurred, for example, out in the desert, there would be nothing left behind for us to find."

"Because wildlife would have finished off the body parts?" Miles asked.

"That's right," Sam said.

Cat made a face. "Coyotes and vultures."

"And foxes and ravens and crows, not to mention a jillion insects. They'd make short work of everything," Sam added. "There's more. Beringer was castrated. Both his dick and his balls were cut off."

Miles grimaced. "That indicates a huge level of anger. What happens now?"

"I'm getting help from the Sheriff's Department. We'll take a look around and see if we can find any remains, although I don't think there will be any. We're going to be on the lookout for the hammer. And we're going to try to figure out who hated Beringer enough to go to all the trouble of not only killing him, but also cutting him up and then hiding his body in the wall of your gallery."

"A crime of passion," Miles asked.

"Looks like it," Sam said. He sat back and took a deep breath. "Okay. I'm going. I'm giving this top priority. I don't like it that this *pendejo* threatened you, Cat."

Miles and Cat both nodded.

"Say hi to your wife. I need to reconnect with Julia. Soon, I hope," Cat added.

"Will do. You two stay vigilant. We'll get this figured out."

After Sam Morales had gone, Cat turned to Miles and said, "I forgot to tell him about Mari Spencer. The death weapon was her hammer."

"We will and soon," said Miles. "But I think she was telling the truth about the hammer. Beringer took it from her and kept it. She loved Beringer. I can't see her cutting him up like that, nor would she have any reason to hide him in your gallery wall."

"Yes, it's probably for the best that I forgot. Mari would surely become a suspect. It would be a waste of Sam's time to go chasing after her. I want him chasing after the real killer."

"Yes, I agree."

"Now, how about that bath?" Cat smiled.

Miles shook his head and frowned. "I don't think you can do that without a lot of help from me. I think I'm going to have to undress you and put you in the tub myself." He grinned.

"You're a naughty boy, Sir Miles." She laughed.

"There you go again. Say 'sir' and you laugh."

Cat grew serious. "Look. I think it's pretty clear you and I really like each other. And I think it's safe to say that we're both attracted to each other."

"Yes, indeed, m'lady. I find you attractive in all the ways a man finds a woman attractive."

"Yes," Cat nodded. "But you are leaving soon. If we go down that road, I'll just end up with a broken heart. I don't need that right now. So if you will take me to the bathroom, I will undress myself, take a bath, and then dress myself. Okay?"

"Okay," Miles sighed. His smile was a little sad now. "I understand. I'm on my best behavior as I promised. It will be up to you to decide if we go any further. I'm willing."

Cat nodded. "Please run me a bath. Make it really warm, too. I'm going to soak for a while."

Miles filled the bathtub and carried Cat to the bathroom.

"Call me if you need me," he said just before closing the bathroom door. "And be careful. Don't slip and fall. Or I'll be forced to run in and save you."

"Thank you, Miles." She paused. "Miles, flirting with you is fun."

"I quite enjoy flirting with you, too, m'lady."

Later soaking in the warm water, Cat wondered to herself. When he says he's willing, is Miles saying that he is willing to have a broken heart?

*　*　*

Miles went to his room and stared at his laptop computer. The laptop was turned off, but Miles continued to stare at the screen.

Cat was right. If they became close, if they made love, it would be very difficult for him to leave. But he had responsibilities. He had to leave, at least for a while. He had his dad to think about, too. Miles didn't know how long it would take him to return or if he would ever return. He didn't want to do that to Cat. She had gone through so much recently. A love affair that was cut short would be hard on her. And not knowing if he would ever return would be intolerable.

And Miles realized that it would be hard on him, too. He knew for sure that if they became lovers, it would break his heart to leave her. He had no desire to return to England and start a new job with a broken heart. He sighed in resignation. A broken heart was probably going to happen anyway, no matter how far he and Cat went in their relationship. Was she worth a broken heart? Yes, a thousand times yes.

Miles decided to focus on finding the killer and making sure that Cat was safe. At least he could leave with some peace of mind. And he could start plotting his return to Bisbee.

12 Freddy

The next morning, Cat called the attorney, Jeremy Flores. She explained that the autopsy had come back for Jax Beringer.

"We have a firm identification, and Beringer has been declared a homicide victim. I found proof in Luis's papers that he had loaned Beringer some money. I'd like to know what I have to do to get what is owed us and also confirm our contract regarding his paintings," Cat told him.

"You are considered a creditor for the loan," Jeremy responded. "You can ask the court to open a probate estate and apply for what's yours from Beringer's estate. Or I recommend your attorney do that for you. The problem is, Cat, I am overwhelmed. I don't have time to work on another project. I told you when you were here all the stuff I'm doing now. I'm so sorry. There just are not enough hours in the day."

"What do you suggest?"

"Considering that Beringer apparently had several creditors, I suggest you find an attorney who can take on everyone. Then the attorney can make sure all the creditors get what they are owed at the same time. That will work well for your gallery, actually. The estate executor will no doubt want you to continue selling Beringer's artwork so there will be some money to pay off creditors.

"Any recommendations for an attorney?"

"I'm the only one in Bisbee now. Let me think about that. You may have to go to Sierra Vista or even Tucson to find someone who can handle this."

"Thanks, Jeremy. I'll get started."

Cat said goodbye. She told Miles about her conversation with Jeremy Flores.

"Luis didn't have a back-up attorney?"

"No, I don't think so. Jeremy took care of everything. There really wasn't a need for a second attorney."

She sat in silence for a few minutes. "I'm a little reluctant to hire just anyone. I think I'm going to call my family in Nogales. One of my cousins, or second cousins, told me that my cousin Frankie was in Tucson now working for a private investigator. He may know someone."

Cat retrieved her phone and began calling her family members in Nogales, Sonora, then Nogales, Arizona, then Tucson.

Miles was listening to her switch back and forth between Spanish and English. He understood everything. He was grinning the entire time.

Cat was watching him.

"Why do you look so happy? Because you understand both languages?" she asked.

"Yes, but it's more than that. My dad is the only family member I have left now. I don't have any siblings. My parents were both only children. So I have no cousins. As I told you, Mum died a couple of years ago. Listening to you is like stepping into the middle of this big family and hearing about everything from the inside. It gives me a really warm feeling."

"Better watch out, Sir Miles. I'll take you with me some time to go visit my family. There are a bunch of them, and they all talk at once. And they'll try to get you to eat way more than you want to eat. And dance with them. You won't just be warm. You'll be hot."

Cat paused. "But you're hot anyway." She giggled.

"Oh," Miles turned pink.

"Sorry. I couldn't help myself. You asked for that."

"I did?" he laughed. "Can I have some more?"

Cat shook her head and grinned. She picked up her phone again and called another number.

"Hey, Frankie! This is your cousin Catalina..... Yeah, I'm back in Bisbee now. What are you up to? I heard you are working for a private investigator? .... You're training to be a private eye yourself. How cool is that? And you're in college, too? You're busy!" The conversation went on for a few minutes. "So you think you know an attorney who could help us?" .... "Okay. I'll wait for your call."

She disconnected and turned to Miles. "He has to ask his boss, Letty Valdez. They are on retainer for an attorney in Tucson. But he wants to ask Letty first to make sure that it's okay with her. It's pretty clear from the way he talks about Letty Valdez that he really admires his boss."

Frankie called back only twenty minutes later. "Letty told me to call Jessica Cameron. I did and Ms. Cameron agreed to take the job. We'll be in Bisbee tomorrow morning. We'll come by your place first. She told me that she needs a list of anyone who has a financial grievance against Jax Beringer."

"I'll get on that right away," Cat said. "But I doubt it will be complete. There's a long list of people with grievances. I'll email the list to you. See you tomorrow, Frankie."

Cat relayed this information to Miles.

"That's good," Miles said. "I'll help you put together the list. Meanwhile, let's go to Jax Beringer's house. Maybe we'll find Freddy Howard."

"Miles, I'm doing so much better this morning. I think if I use the cane and lean on you, I can start walking again."

"If you wish. But let's go slow. You don't want to reinjure your ankle."

"Yes, sir, Sir Miles, sir," she laughed.

He shook his head. "Cheeky girl. What would you say if you met the Queen?"

"I'd say, 'Howdy, Miss Lizzie.'"

Miles rolled his eyes. "Let's hope you never meet Her Majesty."

* * *

Miles and Cat decided to drive to Beringer's house in his rental car, or at least park as close as possible so he could save Cat a walk. That meant going down Tombstone Canyon, then up one of the narrow, winding roads along the mountainside, then onto an even narrower road. He found a place to park about the length of a block from Beringer's house.

Miles helped Cat to steady herself on her two feet. She used the cane for support on one side and her hand on Miles's arm on the other. They walked slowly to Jax Beringer's house. It was a one-story bungalow with a tiny yard, on the side of the mountain. A lovely view of Tombstone Canyon could be seen from the front of the house, and there were neighbors on both sides.

Miles left Cat and walked up the front steps of the house. He knocked. No answer.

"Let's go around back," he suggested. Miles helped Cat to slowly navigate the steps at the side of the house that went to the back. There, they found a flagstone terrace with flowering plants in big pots, a table and some chairs.

Miles helped Cat into a deck chair. He knocked on the back door, then peered in a large window on the back wall.

"Looks like Beringer's studio is located here. I see a large room with several windows and it looks like there's a skylight, too. I see a big painting against one wall. It's not finished. There are patches of unpainted canvas. There's a big table with things on it like cans of paint and brushes and all that artist stuff."

"No sign of anyone?"

"No."

"But someone has been watering these plants. They aren't cacti. They need regular watering." Cat pointed to the flowering plants.

At that moment, they both heard footsteps at the side of the house. Someone was coming.

Freddy Howard appeared at that moment. He froze when he saw Cat and Miles.

"Hello, Mr…., Cat's voice was calm. "Mr. Howard."

"Miss Miranda," he smiled hesitantly. "You learned my real name." He glanced at Miles.

"This is Miles Trevelyan. He and I are working together to figure out what is going on regarding the situation with Jax Beringer. We'd like to know why you gave me a false name, why you didn't tell me you are married to Jax Beringer, and why you want to buy my art gallery." Cat's voice was firm and assertive.

"I'm not married to Jax anymore. He divorced me a little more than two years ago, and he moved to Arizona. He cut off all ties with me. It was only recently that I learned that he was here in Bisbee. I came out to see if there was any chance of reconciliation."

"You are aware, aren't you, that someone murdered Jax?"

Howard's face fell. His eyes filled with tears. "Yes. When I first arrived, I learned that he had disappeared. I went to your gallery hoping to connect with him through you. I was willing to buy the gallery just to keep a relationship with Jax and his art, too. You probably know that I have a gallery in southern California. I've done quite well there. Then I heard through the grapevine just yesterday that he was dead. Someone killed him." He wiped away his tears.

"Why are you here at his house?"

Freddy pulled up a chair and flopped down in it. He put his head in his hands. He sighed and looked at Cat and Miles.

"I came here first thinking that there might be a chance he would show up. I wanted to be here if that happened. Then when I heard he was dead, I just wanted…." he paused. "I wanted to be where he had been for a while. Sleep in his bed. Eat in his kitchen. Look at his art. I know it's silly, but I desperately loved him. It tears me up to know that he's gone. I'm still trying to figure out why he left me. Why he divorced me. Why he didn't love me anymore." Tears reappeared in Freddy's eyes.

"Do you have any idea who might have killed him?"

"Not a clue." He looked at Cat. "I hope the bastard gets caught and sent to prison."

"You seemed to be especially interested in the large painting titled 'Kissed.' What was that about?" Cat asked.

"I don't know really. It was so unlike all his other his paintings. I mentioned that at the time. It didn't even look like his work. Do you think he was in love with someone? Did he create that painting for someone?"

"I don't know."

"Do you know anything about it?"

"I just returned to Bisbee this past week. I only met Jax once and very briefly. So I don't know much about the painting 'Kissed.' My brother never spoke of it. All I know is that Jax's body was found in the wall behind that painting."

Freddy's eyes grew wide. "Oh my god. You mean he was found in the wall of your gallery? His dead body?" His face was white.

Cat nodded. "We had a water leak, and that's how the body was found. I mean when the plumber opened the wall to fix the leak, he found the body."

"That's awful!" Freddy looked very distressed. "He didn't deserve that, to be treated so disrespectfully in death. He was a good man. I can't understand why anyone would want him dead."

"Why did you ask me about a Hockney painting when you were at the gallery?"

Freddy rubbed his head and face with his hand. He looked exhausted.

"We bought that watercolor together. It was a wedding present to us as a couple. When he divorced me, he claimed it as his own. I didn't argue with him. In fact, I told him to take it. I told him that he could keep it if he really wanted it. At that point, I was still hoping to reconcile. Then I discovered that when he left, he had taken it with him. I don't know what happened to it. It's not here in his house. I asked you because I thought maybe you or your brother might know something about it. Did Jax give it to you to sell?"

"No," Cat said. Her answer was honest. The painting was collateral on a loan, not for Luis to sell. Freddy Howard didn't know about the loan.

"Maybe he sold it already," he said.

"Why did you keep your room at the hotel if you're staying here?" Miles asked.

"I didn't want to draw attention to myself. I didn't want anyone to know that I was staying here."

"What are you going to do now?" Cat asked.

"Go home to Los Angeles, I guess," Howard answered. He looked dejected.

"I suppose that's what we should do, too, now, Miles," Cat said, turning to him.

"Yes, I don't think there's much more we can do here." Their goal had been to find Freddy Howard, and they had achieved that.

Howard stayed in his deck chair, his head in his hands.

They said goodbye to Howard. Miles helped Cat down the side stairs to the street.

* * *

"While we're here, Miles, let's go visit one of the neighbors."

"Good idea. How about that house that's on a slightly higher level? I bet the residents can see into Jax's back yard."

"We need to go out to the street, then up that other flight of stairs."

"I'm going to carry you up the stairs."

"Oh, Miles, don't baby me. I can do it."

"It's me we're babying this time. It makes me happy to have you in my arms."

"Oh gosh, Miles, I don't know what to say," Cat said, "Okay. If you insist."

"Will you cuddle up to me like you did earlier?"

"Oh, hush!"

Miles picked her up and started up the stairs. Cat put her arms tightly around him. She began kissing his neck.

"Blimey," Miles whispered.

Cat kissed his cheek.

He groaned.

"What's wrong, Sir Miles?" she giggled.

He sighed. They were at the top of the stairs now. He didn't put her down.

"Miles, we have arrived. You may put me on the ground now. Thank you."

He looked at her, consternation on his face. "Are you sure?"

She nodded. "I'm sure."

Miles sat Cat down on her feet. Then he pulled her roughly toward him. He kissed her hard on her mouth. Then he let her go.

"Oh, Sir Miles is misbehaving." She grinned.

"You started it." He was frowning.

"Sorry, Miles. I'm the one who's misbehaving."

"I like it when you misbehave." He had a very pained look on his face.

"I'm serious. I shouldn't have done that."

Now that she was standing on her own, Cat looked around.

"Let's go knock on that door."

Only a few minutes later, they were sitting in the living room of Mrs. Mary Erik. They quickly learned that Mrs. Erik was a widow. She and her husband had moved to Bisbee from the Chicago area eight years earlier. Mr. Erik died the previous year.

"I'm so happy you knocked on my door," Mrs. Erik said. "I don't get many visitors. I get really lonely sometimes. Would you like some coffee or tea?"

"Tea would be lovely. Do you have any English black tea?" Miles said.

Mrs. Erik giggled. "Do you know what my dear husband used to say? He said, 'If I had a British accent'…like yours, Mr. Trevelyan…'I could have my own harem.'"

Cat laughed.

Miles turned pink.

Mrs. Erik went to the kitchen to make tea.

"Do you have a harem, Sir Miles?" Cat grinned at him.

"*No!*" Miles frowned. "What shall we ask her?"

"Let's just see what she's seen and heard. If she's by herself and doesn't have much to do, she may have seen quite a bit."

Mrs. Erik returned shortly with tea in a pot and cups on a platter plus cream and sugar. She poured for them all.

"Hmmm…," Miles said as he sipped the tea, "delicious."

Mrs. Erik beamed.

Cat spoke first. "Mrs. Erik, we're looking into the death of Jax Beringer who was your neighbor, right?"

"That's right. He lives below me. Or I mean he lived below me. I heard that they found his body."

Cat nodded. "I'll be frank you with you." She had the feeling that Mrs. Erik was well plugged into the Bisbee gossip scene and would love for Cat to be frank.

Mrs. Erik leaned forward. "Yes?"

"Someone has threatened me. Miles and I ran the Great Stair Climb. At staircase six, some man jumped out, assaulted me and threatened to kill me. We also had someone try to run us off the road."

Mrs. Erik gasped. "Oh, that's terrible! Are you okay?"

"I twisted my ankle. Miles has been helping me get back on my feet." She gestured to Miles. "We were wondering if you saw anything unusual at Jax's place before he disappeared, or after for that matter."

"There's been a man staying there the past two or three days."

Cat smiled to herself. And Freddy Howard thought no one knew he was there.

"Yes, we know about him. I mean before that. Did Jax have a lot of visitors? Did you see him get into a conflict with anyone? Or anything noteworthy?"

Mrs. Erik sat back in her seat. She stared off into the distance, thinking.

"He had a lot of female visitors. The entire time he's been living in that house, he had lady friends come over and spend the night. There was one in particular about two months ago who stayed frequently over the course of a few weeks. She's that young carpenter girl."

"Mari Spencer?"

"That's right. She spent the night quite often. Then one day they had a big fight. Jax didn't yell very much actually. He said something to her, and she became very upset. She started crying and yelling. I took a peek over the fence at that point. She was sobbing. She threw something at him. He caught it, and he laughed at her. She was upset, but he just shrugged his shoulders and walked away. Very dismissive. She left. I haven't seen her there since then."

Miles said, "Have you seen any other regular visitors? Or anyone having a particularly serious conflict with Beringer?"

Mary Erik was quiet for a short time.

"Yes, now that you mention it, he had a huge fight with a man. I'm going to guess this was earlier in the summer. It was pretty hot that day. They were outside yelling at each other."

"Could you get the drift of the conversation?" Cat asked.

"I only got fragments of sentences, not enough to understand exactly what the problem was all about. There was something about Jax owing a lot of money to the other man. And the man also warned Jax to stay away from his wife. I heard that pretty clearly."

"Do you have any idea who this man was?" Cat asked.

"Yes, he lives here in Bisbee. I can't think of his name right now. But I do remember Jax laughing when he said that about the wife. Jax said he already got what he wanted from the man's wife. Jax mentioned something about how he'd done a painting for the man's wife to remember their relationship. I mean Jax and the wife's relationship. Jax told the man to look in the gallery for the painting with kissable lips."

She looked at Miles and smiled. He returned her smile.

Cat didn't know whether to laugh or get annoyed. Mary Erik must be nearly eighty years old. She mentions kissable lips, and then she looks at Miles and smiles at him like that. Well, Cat said to herself, the old lady has good taste in men.

"Please continue," Miles said.

"This really enraged the other man. He yelled at Jax in a loud voice. He said he'd be back and get what was his. He said again that Jax owed him money." She paused. "Oh, I remember. His last name is Fuller."

Cat's eyes narrowed. She looked at Miles, then back at Mary Erik.

"You mean Nolan Fuller?" she asked.

"That's right. He has a wife named Helen. They haven't lived here very long. Maybe two years at most. They stick to themselves. I don't know them well at all."

Cat nodded.

"Would you like more tea, Mr. Trevelyan?" Mary Erik said, smiling at Miles.

"Yes, please. And call me Miles," he returned her smile. He held up his cup and Mary Erik filled it.

For another fifteen minutes, they sat politely and chatted with Mrs. Erik. She asked them both a lot of questions about what they had been doing, what they each were going to be doing, what they thought about this and that. Clearly she liked conversing with people and didn't get much of a chance to do so. Cat steered her away from talking about Luis. It was still too painful for Cat to talk about him.

"Miles, are you going to be living here now?" Mrs. Erik asked.

"No, I have to return to England. I have a teaching job waiting for me."

"Oh, that's too bad." She looked at Cat with sadness on her face. "You're going to miss him, aren't you, dear?"

Cat nodded. "Yes. I'll miss Miles a lot." She didn't look at Miles. She was afraid tears would come. She decided to change the subject.

"Mrs. Erik, while I'm here, I wonder if I could interest you in a volunteer project. Do you like working with infants and small children?"

"Oh, yes. I love children, and I especially love babies."

"There an orphanage across the border in Naco, Sonora, that could use some volunteer help. They are looking for senior citizens to come in and provide nurturing for the children, especially the infants."

"What do you mean by that?" Mrs. Erik asked. She looked very interested.

"Babies need to be held and talked to in order to thrive. If they stay in their cribs all the time without any social interaction or mothering, they don't thrive at all. They develop all kinds of health problems, mental and physical. It's terribly sad. So the orphanage is looking for seniors to come in and just hold the babies, rock them, and sing or talk to them."

"That's all? I can do that! I even know a little Spanish. I could communicate with the orphanage workers. But I only know songs in English."

Cat grinned. "The babies won't care what language you choose. They just want to be held and loved."

"Yes, I'm interested."

"Then when I get home, I'll call you with a contact name and number, and you can arrange an appointment to visit the orphanage. It will be up to you to decide how many hours each week you want to be a granny to those orphans."

Cat stood. "Time for us to go. Thank you so much for all the help."

As they were leaving, Miles took Mary Erik's hand in his, and he leaned over and kissed her on the cheek. She blushed profusely.

As they slowly walked back to the car, Miles asked Cat, "Is all that true about the orphanage babies?"

"Yes, it's true. Sad, but true."

"She'll be perfect at being a granny. And it will keep her busy and not so lonely. You are a very kind person to tell her about the orphanage, Catalina Amalia Miranda."

"And you like to flirt with women, Sir Miles, even old ladies." She grinned at him.

Miles shrugged his shoulders. "Sometimes a woman needs a little male attention." He raised his eyebrows and cocked his head when he looked her.

Cat laughed. "You're funny. Let's go home now, eat something, and plan our next move."

13 Helen

Cat and Miles went home. Cat immediately called Mrs. Erik and gave her a contact name and number at the local Catholic Church.

"Let me know how it goes. I bet those babies are going to love having you as a granny," Cat added. "You also may have to hug a toddler or two." They spoke for a few minutes. Cat said goodbye and joined Miles at the kitchen table for lunch.

"I've been thinking about Jax Beringer. That bloke was a real wanker," Miles said. He had a frown on his face.

"Wanker?" Cat smiled. "No, don't tell me. I bet that means *pendejo*, right?"

"Close enough. Jax Beringer was a contemptible person. He used that painting again and again to humiliate people."

Cat nodded. "I actually like the painting. All those sexy lips."

Miles looked surprised. He grinned.

Cat continued, "But you're right. Jax used it against people. I'm really glad I don't have to deal with him."

"Odd that Freddy Howard thought so highly of him."

Cat shrugged her shoulders. "Love is blind."

They were silent for a while, both contemplating the dead man Jax Beringer.

"Could you use a little kip now? You need to rest," Miles said. "Oh, I mean a little siesta."

"Yes, I could use a nap. I guess all the stress and getting hurt has made me pretty low energy. Do you think we have time for that?"

"Certainly."

"Later this afternoon, we'll go see Helen Fuller," Cat said, "and anyone else we can think of. I heard that Beringer screamed at one of the librarians at the public library. And there are merchants up and down Tombstone Canyon that we can talk to. And different workers like Eric, my plumber."

"And learn more about what a wanker he was."

"What does that word mean anyway? 'Wanker'? Is that a made up word?"

Miles looked at her. "You look so innocent. You really don't know?"

"No. I don't know."

"It refers to…you know…."

Cat smiled. "You're turning pink. Must be something sexual, right?"

Miles nodded.

"Okay. Don't say. Just show me."

He grimaced. He made an up-and-down gesture low on his torso with his cupped hand.

Cat laughed out loud. "A wanker is a dude who jacks off a lot?"

"Yes, although I believe the proper term is 'masturbate.'" He was smiling again. "When I'm around you, I don't feel very much like a serious, scholarly intellectual from Oxford University."

"No? So what do you feel like?"

"I better not say."

"You feel like that dude who likes hot and sweet?"

He nodded. "You understand me completely."

"Actually I kind of feel that way, too. I'm giving that outcome some serious consideration."

"That's good news. Keep thinking, m'lady, and you'll come to the correct conclusion."

Cat stood up. "Okay. I'm going to go have a little siesta. What are you going to do?"

Miles frowned. "I don't know. Maybe read a book?"

"Don't take that too far, Sir Miles. I like the Oxford intellectual a lot, but I think I like the hot and sweet dude even better."

"Want me to carry you up the stairs?" He paused and smiled. "Please."

"No. I can manage." She patted him on the shoulder as she passed by. "*Hasta pronto,*" she said. See you soon.

* * *

When Cat awoke from her nap an hour later, she found Miles on his bed, a book open on his chest. He was sound asleep.

She sat on his bed and began bouncing up and down. Miles opened his eyes with a start. When he saw it was Cat, he smiled.

"What are you doing?" He stretched.

"I'm waking you up. Come on, lazy bones. Get up. I'll go make you some coffee."

While they were drinking coffee, Cat said, "I want to go see the Fullers first." She pointed to a map. "Let's drive there so I won't have to go up staircases."

"That's disappointing," Miles made a sad face. "I wanted to carry you."

It took them only a few minutes to arrive at the Fuller place. Miles left the car and knocked. No answer. He returned to the car.

"We can come back here later. Let's try a different place."

"My ankle feels normal. I don't hurt at all. I want to try walking. I think that elastic bandage is really helping."

"Let's take it easy, though. You can use your cane. If you start hurting, I can carry you again." He smiled.

"You have an ulterior motive, Sir Miles. You just want me to kiss your neck again."

"Can you blame me?"

They went down one of the Bisbee staircases to arrive on the main street that meandered through Tombstone Canyon.

"Let's go to the library first," Cat said.

They found the Copper Queen Library in the heart of Bisbee.

"We're really proud of our library. It was founded in the nineteenth century and moved into this building in 1907," Cat said.

"What a beautiful building," Miles said.

The library was housed on the second floor of an elegant older stone building with high windows and ceilings. There was a deck on one side with arched openings. They could see people sitting there in chairs, reading.

"I see there's a lift."

"Elevator? Oh, let's go up the stairs."

The wide flight of stairs took them directly into the library.

"It's just as beautiful inside," Miles said. "Look at all the woodwork. I love libraries."

"Of course you do," Cat laughed.

"I love books."

"Of course you do. You like those hot and sweet books, right?"

"I should never have told you that," he whispered. "You'll tease me forever." He grinned. "You better watch out, Señorita, I'm irresistible to women when I'm in the library."

"I'll keep that in mind."

They went to the main desk. Cat told the clerk behind the main desk that they were hoping to speak to someone about Jax Beringer. She referred to an "incident" in the library that she'd heard about from a friend.

The director of the library, a tall, dark-haired woman came out of an office.

"Hello, I'm Laura Wilson. How can I help you?" She had a friendly smile.

Cat introduced herself and Miles. She explained, as she had earlier to Mary Erik, that she had been assaulted and that she and Miles were attempting to find out as much about Jax Beringer as possible because they believed there was a tie between Beringer and the assault.

"We don't know why someone is after me. We're pretty sure there's a connection to Beringer, but we don't know what it is."

"Yes, we heard about his death and about how his body was found in the wall of your gallery. We hope this all gets straightened out and for you to be safe. We were all excited about the gallery opening again," Laura Wilson said.

"Thank you. I hope that myself," Cat said. "We're going around talking to anyone who has had a conflict with Beringer. We want to piece everything together."

"Well, I can describe the conflict, but I'm afraid it will be typical for the kinds of conflicts Beringer got into. The conflict involved money. He had an overdue fine on a book that he had checked out and was late in returning. The fine was maybe a dollar or not even that. He argued and said he didn't have to pay it. He started yelling right away. I came out and told our clerk to just let him go. It wasn't worth fighting over a dollar."

"That's not much of a fine," Cat said. "Why do you suppose he became so angry?"

"He was an angry man. He went ballistic really fast about everything."

Cat nodded. "What was the book he checked out?"

"Oh, I'm sorry. We don't really reveal our patrons' reading preferences. That's considered private."

"Anything else you can tell me?"

"Not really. He rarely came in to our library."

"Thanks so much. We'll be going."

Miles said, "Thank you, Ms. Wilson. You have a lovely library. I'm honored to visit. I hope to return and explore your collection."

"Come back anytime, Mr. Trevelyan."

Cat and Miles left the library and went up the street to a ceramics shop. The front of the shop had shelves with lovely glazed ceramic pots and cups. A man and woman, both in their twenties, were at the back of the large room. They were both at ceramic wheels throwing clay to make more pots.

The young man came forward smiling. "How can I help you?"

Cat explained why they were there.

The young man frowned. "Yeah, Beringer was here some months back. He's a dick. He tried to get a set of coffee cups from us for half off. He said there were flaws in the clay. Bullshit. On top of that, he hit on my wife." The young man gestured to the woman who had stopped her wheel and was listening.

"We're Willow and Michael," she said with a smile.

"And we're Cat and Miles," Cat gestured to Miles. "So he tried to get your wares for half off?"

"Yeah," Michael said. "Everybody had that problem with Beringer. He either tried to get a big reduction on the price or better yet, get everything for free."

"Do you suppose he had financial problems?" Miles asked.

"Maybe. Rumor was that he had a gambling problem. There were stories that he went across the border to gamble and usually came up short. That may explain why he tried to get freebies everywhere. Or it could just be that he was a dick." Michael frowned.

Cat grinned. "Everyone seems to think that. I only met him once."

"We ended up giving him the set of cups. I told him to never come back to our shop," Michael's face changed. "Hey, is it true that the plumber found Beringer's body in the wall of your gallery?"

"True."

Michael grimaced. "I'm sorry for you, Cat, but not for him."

"Thank you. By the way, when I open the gallery again, I'll be looking for some ceramic art. Big one-of-kind pots with surface design. Or better yet, sculptural work."

"Really?" Michael brightened. "Willow and I both do art pieces."

"Then come on by and we'll talk about it. I hope to open the gallery soon."

Miles and Cat left the shop with everyone smiling.

"You're going around spreading good cheer," Miles said.

"Let's hope so. We need some good cheer."

"Gambling debts may explain his behavior," Miles said.

"Yes. This may be a matter of finding his debtors. Let's go back to the Fullers' house."

* * *

They walked to the steps that would take them up to the Fuller home.

"Do me a favor, Ms. Miranda. I need more exercise. Would you allow me to carry you up these steps?" Miles asked. His tone of voice was serious, and he was frowning.

Cat laughed. "I think you want me to kiss your neck."

"I need the exercise, thank you very much." He bent down and scooped her up.

Cat did as expected. She kissed his neck and cheek repeatedly.

Miles was smiling when they arrived at the top of the staircase. "Thank you, m'lady. That was very good exercise. Very stimulating."

They knocked on the Fullers' door. This time, a female voice called out, "Who is it?"

"Cat Miranda," Cat said. "I just need a few minutes of your time."

The door opened but just a crack. "What do you want?"

"Can Miles and I come in for a few minutes? Remember me? You asked me about buying my art gallery."

Helen Fuller opened the door. "Okay. Come in, but just for a minute." She stepped back.

As Cat and Miles entered her house, Cat looked at her. Helen Fuller had a black eye and a badly bruised cheek.

"Are you okay?" Cat asked. She'd seen evidence of abuse before when she volunteered at the women's shelter. She recognized the signs of physical abuse in Helen Fuller.

"Yes, I'll be okay before this day is over." She gestured to the couch. They sat down.

"Is your husband here?"

"No. I don't know where he is. He didn't come home last night."
Cat noticed two large suitcases near the door.

"Are you going somewhere?"

"Yes," Helen Fuller said in a firm voice. "I've had it. My husband beats me when he's angry. I've had enough. I'm leaving."

"Where are you going?"

"I'm not sure yet. And I won't tell anyone because I don't want Nolan following me. As if he would anyway. He doesn't care about me. He just wants money."

"Money?" Cat cocked her head, a confused look on her face.

"Yeah," she hesitated. "I should warn you, Miss Miranda."

Miles leaned forward, watching her intently.

"Warn me about what?" Cat asked.

"Nolan has become more and more unpredictable. He wants your gallery. He wants that painting. The one called 'Kissed.' He wants everything."

"I don't understand."

"Nolan and I knew Jax Beringer in California. We were already living in Bisbee at the time. We were planning on opening a gallery here similar to your gallery. We were going to cultivate a national clientele, sell artwork online and also have a highly-regarded gallery here in Bisbee. We came up with a short list of artists to start with. We went to Los Angeles to see a couple of them. We approached Jax to see if he was interested in working with us. He said yes. This was around the time that he left that man he was married to, Freddy Howard. Jax was in the process of ending his relationship, both business and personal, with Freddy Howard. Jax told us that he was moving to Bisbee, and he wanted to be our star artist. Only a month later, he moved here."

"And you signed a contract to represent him?"

"No. I'm sorry to say that there was no signed contract on paper. We had what my husband called a 'verbal contract.' Jax insisted that we give him a huge financial incentive. Only then would he agree to be our artist. I warned my husband about this, but he didn't listen. Jax came here to Bisbee and right away, he started putting us off. There was always some excuse as to why he didn't sign a real contract. And then I made a mistake."

"*You* made a mistake? What do you mean?"

"I'd call it an indiscretion. Jax and I had a brief affair." She shook her head. "Jax was so charming. Nolan was never nice to me, always complaining, and he would hit me if he didn't get what he wanted. I fell for Jax Beringer."

"And your husband was really angry when he found out?"

"Angry isn't the word. He was livid. At first he was hysterical, yelling and screaming. He beat me repeatedly. Then he became very quiet, and he wouldn't talk to me at all. I think now he was planning something."

"Planning what?" Miles asked in a soft, encouraging tone of voice.

"Revenge."

"Why did you come to me and ask to buy the gallery?" Cat asked.

"Nolan found out that Jax had signed a contract with your brother. That enraged Nolan. When your brother died, Nolan thought that if we bought out your gallery, we would own Jax Beringer and his artwork, too. It would have wiped us out financially to buy you out. We'd already lost all that money that Nolan had given Jax, money that Jax never returned. Jax refused to honor the verbal agreement. But when Nolan found out about Jax and me, Nolan's anger and desire for revenge took him over the top. He wasn't thinking clearly. I don't know how we could have run the gallery with no money. Buying your gallery was a crazy idea. But I went along with it because Nolan would have beaten me if I hadn't."

"Nolan persisted?"

"He did. He was a mad man. Then Jax did something that insulted my husband beyond words. Jax told Nolan to go look at the painting 'Kissed' in your gallery. Jax said he created that painting to remind us all that Jax had taken possession of me."

Cat glanced at Miles. He was frowning and shaking his head.

"And your husband went nuts?"

"Yes, and that meant he beat me again. Then your brother died, and Jax disappeared." She looked at Cat straight in the eye. "I think my husband killed Jax Beringer."

"Wow. That's quite a story. You have no idea where your husband is now?" Cat asked.

"No, but I'm getting out of here before he returns."

"What do you think he's planning now?" Miles asked.

"I don't know how the law works in these kinds of cases. I'm not a lawyer. But he said something once that makes me think he's still trying to get control of Jax's art. And now that Jax is dead, his artwork might be worth even more."

"What did your husband say?" Miles asked.

"Nolan said that if something were to happen to Cat, and if Cat had no inheritors, then my husband might be able to convince a court that he had a legally binding agreement with Jax. That means he would try to get Jax's art away from your gallery and claim that he has the right to sell it at a profit."

"If something happened to Cat…" Miles repeated. "That sounds ominous."

Helen Fuller stood up. "It *is* ominous." She looked directly at Cat. "If he can't scare you into selling the gallery to him, then he may try to eliminate you altogether. My husband is capable of anything. I honestly think this whole thing with Jax has made him a psycho. I'm scared of him. He'll do anything to get what he wants."

Cat and Miles stood up, too.

"Thank you for seeing us and giving us this information," Cat said.

All three left the Fullers' house at the same time. Miles helped Helen Fuller load her luggage into her car. Then he and Cat watched her drive away.

Cat looked up at Miles. She took his hand in hers.

"The good news is that I think we know now who is causing all the problems."

Miles nodded.

"The bad news is that he's targeting me."

"We need to talk to Sam Morales and the Sheriff's Department, too. They can start looking for Fuller. Meanwhile, I'm sticking to you like glue."

Cat leaned into his chest. "Thank you, Sir Miles. I'm so glad you're here. I would be in such trouble if you weren't."

Miles put his arms around Cat. "It's very possible that Fuller was the one who attempted to break into your home that first night I was here."

Cat nodded. Her face and voice were serious. "Yes. I can't think of anyone else it might have been."

She pulled out her phone and made a quick call to Sam Morales. After telling him what Helen Fuller had shared, Morales said he would alert the Sheriff's Department and get an APB out on Fuller. After she hung up, she shared this with Miles.

"The cops broadcast an 'All Points Bulletin,' or APB, with info about a suspect or a person of interest. Law enforcement will start looking for that person or persons with the goal of bringing them in for questioning."

Miles nodded. "Good. I hope they find him and fast." They walked a little further. "So what do we do now?"

"Let's go see Amanda. You can get one of those beers you like. She may have some news for us."

"Great idea. But it's stout, not beer."

"Fine. Then my favorite bloke can have a pint of stout."

"Brilliant, m'lady."

* * *

Fifteen minutes later, they were seated at the bar in the Star Tavern. The place was almost empty. Miles was happily sipping his stout.

Amanda was behind the bar, drying glasses with a white towel.

"So what's new?" she asked.

Cat recounted all the conversations they'd had, and their conclusion that Nolan Fuller may be the man behind their problems.

"Fuller has been coming in here for a couple of years," Amanda said. "As I mentioned before, he was always alone and his interactions with other customers were minimal. But I can say that his behavior had become somewhat more erratic the past few months. He seemed angry, and if anyone crossed him, he would yell and threaten to start a fight."

"What do you mean by 'crossed him'?" Cat asked.

"Little things. Once a billiard ball got away from one of the players and ended up bouncing off Fuller's table. It came close to hitting his glass of beer. He got really angry about that."

"Do you have any idea where he might be now?" Miles asked.

"No," Amanda answered immediately. "He hardly ever spoke to me. And I heard very little gossip about him. However, I can ask around. Maybe he has some kind of hideaway out in the desert or something."

Miles nodded.

"I have some advice for you, if you don't mind," Amanda said to Cat.

"Please go ahead. We need all the help we can get right now."

"The Día de los Muertos celebration is coming up day after tomorrow. Most of the festivities happen at night. With everyone dressed up in costume, it seems like a perfect time for Fuller to disguise himself. He may try to go after you then, Cat. You best be very careful." She turned to Miles. "You'll be with Cat, right?"

"Absolutely yes. I won't leave her side."

"Good. I'll call you if I learn any more about Fuller's whereabouts."

Miles finished his stout, and they headed home.

* * *

Later that night, lying in bed and staring at the ceiling, Miles Trevelyan wished for the first time in his life that he had a lot of money. If money were no object, he would hire a team of security experts to protect Cat around the clock, to protect and keep her safe from any harm.

But he didn't have a lot of money. He probably never would have a lot of money. Miles didn't care about money. He loved history, he loved his work, and he loved books. He thought maybe he loved Cat, too. He didn't know if he would be able to leave her unprotected when it came time for him to go. Staying here meant not showing up for his job at the university in Essex. Not showing up meant breaking his contract. He would get a reputation as being unreliable and irresponsible. That kind of reputation could ruin a career as an academic. How would he support himself if he couldn't get a teaching job?

Even if he left under the best circumstances, meaning if Cat were safe, how could he really leave her? His feelings for her were strong.

Miles sighed. Once, sometime ago, he had looked up the origin of the phrase "horns of a dilemma." It was Greek, of course. The Greek logician Phædrus had come up with some logical alternatives to deal with an angry bull, an angry bull ready to charge. None of the alternatives was good. That's how Miles felt now. An angry, psychotic bull was ready to charge. How could Miles protect the lovely Señorita Catalina Amalia Miranda from those lethal horns?

14 Frankie and Jessica

The next morning, as they were drinking coffee on the outdoor deck upstairs, Miles noticed that Cat was staring at him.

He looked at her, confused. "What?"

"You Brits all have messy hair. You never comb your hair," Cat said.

"Really? What are you talking about?"

"Boris Johnson, your president, has messy hair."

"Prime Minister. Boris Johnson is Prime Minister. For now, anyway."

"Whatever. He has messy hair. Also that guy who was speaker of the House. The one that yelled 'Order!' all the time."

"John Bercow?"

"Yeah, that's him. Same with him. No combing. No brushing. His hair kind of sticks out. Some of the women politicians are like that, too. Messy hair."

"Does that bother you?"

"No. I think it's kind of cute really."

"Cute?" Miles was grinning now. "Do you think I'm cute?"

"Yeah."

"What about debonair, suave and irresistibly sexy?"

Cat shrugged her shoulders nonchalantly. "Yeah, that, too," she said casually.

Miles laughed. "For the record, I think you're cute, too, even though your hair is quite lovely and not at all messy. You're not debonair or suave, but you are definitely sexy. Irresistibly sexy."

"Thank you, Sir Miles. Actually, you look a little like that lead singer for the American band Spoon. You have strawberry blond hair like his. What I mean is, you don't look like him, but you have his messy hair. Or he has your messy hair. Same color. And sticking out."

"You're very interested in my hair."

"I'm thinking about making you up for Día de los Muertos."

"Making me up?"

"Making up your face so you'll look like a dead ghost."

"Ghosts are usually dead."

"You know what I mean. Like a traditional sugar skull look for Día de los Muertos."

"Sounds lovely."

"You can wear my brother's big Mexican hat and his dark jacket. The jacket was too big for him so I think it will fit you just fine. You're too tall for his pants. I'll have my face painted, too. Everyone will be face-painted for Día de los Muertos. There'll be a parade and a street party, too. We'll drink and dance and have fun."

Miles grinned. "I think I'm going to like being a dead ghost."

"Good. Consider it a done deal. You're a dead ghost now. I'll make you up tomorrow for the festivities." Cat sipped her coffee. "Oh, yeah. Let's not forget. My cousin Frankie Miranda is coming this morning with the attorney, Jessica Cameron."

"Very good, m'lady."

* * *

Cat waved to Frankie as he drove up her street. She and Miles hurried down the stairs and out the back door to greet them. Cat had never met Jessica Cameron. That Cameron had been recommended by Frankie, and by Frankie's boss, private investigator Letty Valdez, made Cat think that Jessica was a good choice to help her with her troubles.

Frankie Miranda and Jessica Cameron got out of the car.

"Hey, Frankie," Cat said, as she gave him a hug.

Frankie turned to Jessica. "I'd like to introduce Jessica Cameron. She's an attorney for a big law firm in Tucson. She's famous because she helps out the poor suckers who get screwed by rich people."

Jessica laughed, "That's quite an introduction, Frankie."

"And this is Miles Trevelyan. He's a visiting scholar from Oxford University doing research on the Borderlands." Cat gestured to Miles.

Miles took Jessica's hand. "I look forward to chatting with you, Ms. Cameron."

"Call me Jessica. I want to hear all about your research and all about Oxford, too. I've had an occasional thought about returning to school for a doctoral degree. Oxford University is high on my list."

Cat noticed right away that Frankie and Jessica appeared to have little in common, most obviously in physical appearance.

Jessica had shoulder-length blonde hair and a fair complexion. She was wearing casual but expensive clothing and a Stetson hat, the style known as "open road." High-fashion jeans, plaid flannel shirt, and a light-weight leather jacket as well as some light-weight hiking boots completed her look. She had on makeup, too, noticeably a bright red lipstick. She was pretty, some might even say beautiful.

Frankie was Frankie, a typical member of the Miranda family. He was a small man, five feet six inches and with a slight build. His skin was a warm shade of brown, and he had dark brown hair and eyes like Cat. Tattoos were visible on what could be seen of his arms and his neck. He was wearing that same black fedora hat he'd been wearing the last time Cat saw him.

Cat was about four years older than Frankie. She had known him all his life. For most of that time, he had lived in Nogales, where he grew up. Cat had grown up in Bisbee, gone to university in Tucson and worked in Phoenix. So months often went by when they did not see each other. He was a computer geek, and he had the reputation for being the smartest member of the Miranda family.

"You're running out of space for tattoos. Then what will you do?" Cat smiled at Frankie.

"Accept myself as I am, I guess," he grinned. "And you. Last I heard, you only had one tattoo. When are you going to get some more?"

Cat smiled and nodded. "I'm thinking about it."

She glanced back to see that Miles and Jessica had walked off together in animated conversation. She felt a sudden pang of jealousy at the way they seemed to have hit it off immediately. Worse than that, she realized that she felt inadequate. She and Miles liked to tease each other, and there was a definite sexual tone to the teasing. But could he ever respect her? Ever see her as his intellectual equal? She shook her head. She knew she had a problem with self-confidence. Or more accurately, lack of self-confidence. Her unhappy marriage had played a big role in that. Maybe that's why she felt inadequate. She shook her head. Why was she even thinking about this? Some psycho had threatened to kill her, and she's fretting about Miles and what he thought of her? Stupid. Miles was leaving soon, and she'd never see him again. What did it matter what he thought? She just wished that she didn't like him so much.

Frankie and Cat followed Miles and Jessica into her kitchen.

"Would you like some coffee?" Cat asked.

"No, thank you," Jessica said. "We need to check into our hotel. They're going to give us a private dining room this afternoon where I can meet potential clients. I need some time to organize my notes."

"Where are you staying?"

"The Copper Queen," Jessica said with a smile. "I'm hoping to see one of the resident ghosts."

She was referring to Bisbee's beautiful Copper Queen Hotel, which opened its doors in 1902. There were persistent reports that the hotel was haunted. Tourists loved that.

"And you, Frankie. Want to stay here? We don't have much room, but I can find an air mattress for you if you don't mind sleeping on the floor," Cat said.

"Not to worry," Jessica inserted, before Frankie said anything. "I'm arranging for him to have his own room at the Copper Queen. He's going to be helping me with this project so his room, and mine, too, are business expenses."

Frankie grinned. Cat grinned, too, knowing that Frankie didn't have enough money to spend on any hotel or motel, much less Bisbee's most famous. She was pleased that her cousin would have this experience.

Jessica continued. "We'll have the meeting this afternoon with as many people as we can gather. Frankie will go around and talk to people both before and after the meeting to see who had a grievance with Jax Beringer and who could benefit and make a claim on his estate. After the meeting, I'm going to engage in being a tourist for a bit. This is my first time to come to this part of Arizona. Then Frankie and I will go home tomorrow afternoon. There's a big Día de los Muertos event happening in Tucson, and I don't want to miss it."

Cat nodded. "I'm going to call Carmen Fuentes and ask her to come."

"Yes, I remember her name on the list you sent us," Jessica said. "She says Jax Beringer is the biological father of her child?"

"That's right. She's the one who will need Jax's money most of all," Cat said.

"Let's call Amanda, too," Miles said.

Cat smiled. "Amanda is the owner of the Star Tavern. People tell her things."

"Good. Now while we're here, I'd like very much to see your gallery and your artwork."

Cat led Jessica into the gallery. They went around and looked at artwork in a systematic fashion. Cat told her who the artist was, a little about him or her, and anything she knew about the painting or sculpture. Then they came to Jax Beringer's painting "Kissed."

Cat told Jessica about how Jax Beringer used the painting to embarrass and humiliate those women he'd been involved with, and to goad Nolan Fuller in particular. She also described how the plumber had found Jax's body in the wall behind the painting.

"Everything I've heard about the artist makes me glad I never met him," Jessica said. She stood back a few feet to get a look at the huge painting. "This painting, however, is another matter."

Cat looked at her. "You like it?"

"No. Love, love, love is a more accurate description. It's just fabulous."

Cat was really surprised. "Most people look at it and think it's strange."

"That's because they all knew Beringer. I just see the painting, not the artist. Consider it sold." She turned to Cat with a smile on her face.

Cat saw the look on Jessica's face, and she knew immediately what opposing attorneys must feel when they went against Lawyer Cameron in court. Lovely, charming, and determined to get her own way.

"You haven't asked how much it costs."

"How much?"

"My brother Luis had a price of twenty thousand dollars on it."

"Fine. Can you arrange to have it shipped to Tucson?"

"Yes. Definitely." Cat said. She did her best to not gasp in surprise.

"I just bought a condo in downtown Tucson with floor-to-ceiling windows facing the Santa Catalina Mountains. This painting will be fabulous on the wall opposite the window."

"Okay," Cat said. She didn't really know what to say.

"Send me an invoice, and I'll wire you the money and information on where to deliver the painting. I've got to get going. I'll see you later this afternoon."

With that, Jessica strode to the kitchen where Frankie and Miles were talking about artificial intelligence. "Let's go, Frankie. See ya', Miles." With that, she headed for the car.

Frankie said his goodbyes. "I'll text you with the time and place of the meeting."

As soon as they were gone, Cat turned to Miles.

"You'll never guess what just happened. Jessica Cameron bought that big Beringer painting." She giggled and clapped her hands.

"The one with all the kissing lips?"

"Right. I feel a little guilty. I told her the price was twenty thousand dollars, and she didn't blink an eye. That was the price Luis put on it. Maybe I should have gone down a little?"

"She didn't ask you to lower the price, did she? Anyway, that money will go into Beringer's estate. Carmen's little baby will get a chunk of that."

"Oh, that's good." She nodded. "That makes me feel better. Also our gallery will get a percentage."

Cat couldn't help herself. She reached out and put her arms around Miles. She hugged him hard and then let him go. She could hear his breath come out in a sharp burst.

"Thank you, Miles."

"I didn't do anything."

"You've done a lot, Miles. You make me feel more confident. When I'm around you, I believe in myself more."

Miles nodded. He suppressed a groan. Oh, how on earth was he going to walk away from this woman?

"So now, Sir Miles, we need to make phone calls." She laughed.

"There you go again. Say 'Sir Miles' and you laugh. I think you owe me for your disrespect." He had a serious look on his face, but he was biting his lip so he wouldn't laugh.

"Owe you?" She could barely suppress a grin.

"Yeah, you have to eat lunch with me at Amanda's tavern. I want a stout."

"It's a done deal," Cat said. "We can get the Bisbee gossip mill started about the meeting this afternoon."

* * *

Cat and Miles were eating at the Star Tavern when Cat received a text from Frankie. "The meeting is at four this afternoon," she told Miles. She turned to Amanda who was eating with them. "Can you come, too?"

"I have a half-time employee who is supposed to come in at five. I'll call and see if she can come a little early. But you know, I didn't really have a money issue with Jax Beringer. He paid his tab every time he came in, and he didn't argue with me."

"How did you get him to do that?" Miles asked.

"I told him that if he ever wanted so much as a drop of that imported stout or ale again, he had to pay up. Every time."

Miles and Cat both laughed.

"I completely understand his compliance," Miles said.

"I could take business lessons from you, Amanda." Cat grinned.

"No problem. Happy to help another Bisbee entrepreneur."

Cat and Miles hung out with Amanda for a while. Then they took a stroll around downtown Bisbee. Everywhere they stopped, they told people about the meeting. When they arrived at the Copper Queen just before four o'clock, they were directed to a large private dining room. The room was completely full of people, many of whom Cat knew personally. She saw Carmen Fuentes holding her baby. She was accompanied by one of her brothers.

"Good grief," Cat said. "Jax had a lot of folks pissed off at him."

"Look. There's Frankie and Jessica," Miles said.

Frankie was sitting at a table with Jessica. He had a laptop open in front of him. Jessica had transformed herself into the television image of a high-powered attorney. She was dressed in an elegant navy blue suit with an ivory-colored silk shirt and spiked heels. Her hair was up in a French roll at the back of her head, and she wore dark-rimmed glasses. Other than the bright red lipstick, she looked very serious and very professional. As she spoke to Frankie, he typed on the laptop. He nodded frequently.

The meeting went well. Jessica started by explaining the probate estate process. She talked for about fifteen minutes without stopping and without taking questions.

"We'll try to avoid a lawsuit because that will slow things down," she explained. "I think we can manage this through probate. My goal is to make sure each of you gets what Beringer owes you because you deserve it. What I'll need from each of you are details about your issues with Jax Beringer. Now, I'll take questions of a general nature. If it's about your personal complaint, then we'll deal with that later, one-by-one.

When Jessica said that, everyone started talking at once. She raised her hand, and everyone fell silent.

"General questions only."

Three people raised their hands. One asked her how long the probate process would take. Another asked if Mexican nationals could get in on the process, and a third asked how much they would have to pay her.

"Regarding how long it will take, I think probably a few months at most. Regarding Mexican nationals, I'll look into that, but I think that won't be a problem at all. Regarding payment for me, that ultimately will come out of Beringer's estate. So you don't have to pay me anything."

When she said that, the crowd murmured. Cat could see a lot of smiles.

Jessica continued, "Now, my assistant Frankie Miranda has a paper handout with a questionnaire. Fill it out and either mail it to my office in Tucson or scan it and email it to Frankie if you have the equipment for that. He's bilingual and the questionnaire is in two languages. So answer in either English or Spanish. Once we read your answers, we'll contact you personally about the specifics of your case. Be sure to give us your correct and current contact information. Then we'll be able to reach you."

At that, Jessica ended the meeting and left the room. Cat saw her heading up the stairs to her room in the Copper Queen.

"Very efficient," Miles said.

"Yes, I think she's a good choice to handle this. And she looks like she's having a good time."

"Jessica is doing what she loves."

* * *

Later that evening, Cat and Miles were sitting on the upstairs outdoor deck. They had just returned from escorting Jessica and Frankie around Bisbee. Cat gave them, and Miles, too, a running commentary on Bisbee past and present.

Now on the deck, Cat and Miles had pushed their chairs close together. They were holding hands.

"I've been thinking about this," Miles said. "It seems very odd that Nolan Fuller would give Jax a large amount of money only on the basis of a verbal agreement. That seems incredibly naïve, and Fuller doesn't appear to be a naïve kind of person. We know Jax was bi-sexual. Perhaps he and Fuller had a personal and sexual relationship. Fuller may have become enchanted by Beringer the same way so many women did."

"And then Fuller felt deeply betrayed by Jax, not only for signing a contract with Luis and causing Fuller to lose all that money ….," Cat added.

"…but also for dumping Fuller, and then seducing Fuller's wife," Miles finished.

"Nolan Fuller was eaten up with rage," Cat added. "Helen Fuller didn't mention this because…."

"Maybe she didn't know. She didn't know that her husband had been involved with her lover."

"We may never know what happened," Cat added.

"True. Fuller is the only one who knows, and he's not likely to share that."

"But it could be the origin of his rage."

Miles nodded. "And the cause for a crime of passion."

"So he's obsessed now about getting control of Beringer's paintings."

They fell silent.

Cat finally said, "I'm so glad Jessica bought that painting. Not just for the money, but to get rid of it. It's a good painting, but I don't want it around anymore. I wish we knew what Beringer was really thinking of when he painted it, but we'll never know."

"Jessica's purchasing it is a good resolution. Yes, it's a good painting, and it doesn't deserve to be linked to all this madness. Maybe someday we can go to Tucson. We can visit Jessica's condo and see the painting at home."

Cat nodded. She said nothing. Does that mean Miles is thinking of returning? or of not leaving at all? Talking about the two of them visiting Tucson together made her think of that. Her heart was starting to hurt when she thought of Miles. She squeezed his hand.

Miles lifted her hand to his lips, and he kissed it.

Cat smiled. It was the second time Miles had kissed her, even if it was just her hand. Maybe his promise to behave was eroding. Finally. She was getting a bit tired of a behaving Sir Miles.

15 Día de los Muertos

The next morning, Cat and Miles ate breakfast with Frankie and Jessica at the hotel.

"We're going back to Tucson this afternoon," Jessica said. "I have things to do." She turned to Frankie. "I may send you back here later to do more investigation for me."

Frankie beamed. "That sounds great. You know I'm in training to be a private investigator, so this will be good experience for me."

"If that happens, you can stay with me," Cat said. "Miles is leaving soon. You can sleep in his room." She barely got the words out because thinking about and talking about Miles leaving was painful, but she had to face reality. She glanced at Miles.

He was staring at his coffee cup, frowning.

"Would you like to go with us to Tucson?" Jessica asked Cat.

"No. I'll keep everything locked up tight then. Our police chief Sam Morales said he'd come by and check on me. I'll be okay."

Miles shook his head. His frown deepened. "I wish you weren't so stubborn, Cat."

"I gave this a lot of thought. This is my home, Miles. I don't want to be scared off. I have work to do. I'm planning a grand opening for the gallery soon. Then when my neighbors move, I'll move into the house next door. I'll be busy."

Miles shook his head again. He and Cat had discussed her leaving Bisbee until Nolan Fuller could be found and arrested. Miles knew that Fuller could have fled Bisbee. Maybe that All Points

Bulletin would work, and the police would find him. Or he could still be in Bisbee hiding out, waiting to find Cat alone and vulnerable. But nothing Miles said could convince her. She wouldn't be moved. She refused to leave. And he couldn't stay.

"Okay. I'm going across the border to Naco, Sonora, and behave like a tourist this morning." Jessica stood up from the table and pushed her chair back. "You get busy, Frankie, and I'll meet with you here at two this afternoon. We'll return to Tucson then."

* * *

Cat and Miles returned to the gallery and Cat's home. They barely spoke.

When they arrived, Cat said, "Okay with you if we continue to do the artwork inventory? It goes a lot faster if you and I work together. This won't interrupt your packing?"

"No, I don't have much at all. Packing will only take a few minutes. I'd be happy to help you, m'lady."

They went into the storeroom and began the inventory work. They stopped later for a quick lunch then went back to work all afternoon. They spoke very little to each other.

Cat avoided looking at Miles. She was starting to feel like a fool. She had a history of falling for the wrong guy. Her ex-husband was a bad choice because he was so disturbed. Miles was a bad choice because he lived on the other side of the planet.

She looked over at Miles. He was staring at his laptop screen at the spreadsheet inventory of artworks that he had created. He was so smart and funny and sweet, not to mention really handsome and sexy. Well, Cat, she said to herself, a real fool is someone who doesn't have fun when she can. She knew she'd have a broken heart when he was gone. That was unavoidable. But for now, she wanted to enjoy every minute with Sir Miles.

"Hey, you," she said.

Miles looked up. Cat was smiling broadly at him. "I know you'll be gone soon. I want to enjoy the time I have left with you. So cheer up. We'll have fun this evening."

His face changed from serious concentration, to relief, to a smile. "Thank you, m'lady. I also want to enjoy our time together."

"Let's finish up, get a quick bite to eat, then I'm going to change and make up my face for the Día celebrations. Then I'll do your face. We'll go to the parade, listen to the music, dance a little, and have fun while you're still in Bisbee."

"Do you think you can dance? I'm concerned about your ankle."

"My ankle doesn't hurt at all."

"Let's put the elastic bandage on it anyway to give you maximum stability."

Cat nodded. "Let's go upstairs and do that. Then I'll give you Luis's old jacket and hat, and you can change. I'll change, too."

They ate, and then went to Cat's room. She sat on her bed with her leg stretched out. Miles wrapped the elastic bandage around her ankle.

"You've taken good care of me," Cat said softly.

"I could take better care of you if you would listen to me," he frowned and smiled at the same time. "Hey, I have an idea. Want to go with me to England?" He knew she wouldn't.

Cat shook her head no. She countered, "Do you want to stay here?"

"Yes, I do. But I can't stay just now, Cat. I'll try my best to return."

"We're star-crossed. So let's just have fun while we can." Cat figured she'd never see him again once he was gone.

"As you wish, m'lady."

When Miles finished wrapping her ankle, Cat gave him the heavy black mariachi jacket and hat with elaborate silver trim.

"Meet me downstairs in about twenty minutes. We'll do your face."

Miles dressed quickly in black jeans, a white shirt and the jacket that had belonged to Luis. He went to the kitchen and sat at the table waiting for Cat.

When she appeared, Miles gasped. He stood up grinning. "Oh, what a gorgeous dead ghost you are, m'lady."

Cat was decked out in the style of the traditional Lady Catrina, La Calavera Catrina. Cat swung around, twirling her full, dark skirt. She had on a lovely white embroidered blouse with a gathered neckline that wasn't up to her neck at all. The neckline was quite low, and Miles could see cleavage, much to his great pleasure. He could also see that tattoo that he was so curious about. A butterfly. A tattoo of a butterfly.

Cat's face was made up in the Catrina skull manner, entirely white with dark eyes, painted flower petals around the dark pools of the eyes, with bits of sparkly gold eyeshadow within each petal. The tip of her nose was black, too. Her mouth was a dark purple, almost black, and dark, thin horizontal lines stretched out from the corners of her mouth almost to her ears. There were thin vertical lines along the horizontal lines that were meant to look like stitches on a corpse. On her head was a wreath with brightly-colored paper flowers and ribbons attached.

"You're beautiful, so beautiful," Miles whispered.

Cat laughed. "I'm a dead ghost."

"The most beautiful dead ghost in the world," he said. "I'd better shut up. I'm repeating myself."

"Sit down, and we'll do your face."

Miles sat on a kitchen chair. Cat placed her chair next to his but facing the opposite way. When they were seated, they were close together, side-by-side, facing each other. She handed him a mirror.

Using a brush, Cat covered his face with a very light, almost white foundation. She emphasized the hollows beneath his cheekbones with a slightly darker foundation. With a jumbo eyeliner, she outlined his eyes in a big circle up to his eyebrows above, and almost to his cheekbones, below. The effect was to create eyes set into large pools of black. She put the same dark makeup on the tip of his nose and chin.

Miles loved having her so close. She smelled really good. Her eyes were focused on him. Such lovely dark brown eyes.

"Take a look," she said.

Miles held up the mirror. He looked at himself. He grinned.

"Okay. Now let's do more on your eyes." With a thin liquid eyeliner, she drew a large spider on his forehead above his eyes with its eight legs reaching down onto his nose and face. Next, she drew the horizontal lines out from the corners of his mouth, and vertical lines to indicate stitches.

"Look."

He held the mirror up. "I'm a dead ghost." He grinned.

"Now we're going to transfer some of this dark lipstick to your lips," Cat said. She had this mischievous smile on her face.

"Transfer? Not paint directly?" he asked.

"Transfer."

Cat picked up the tube of dark purple lipstick and applied a thick layer on her own lips. Then she leaned in and kissed Miles, kissed him on the lips in a most sensual manner. She kissed him several times, and he responded with enthusiasm. Then she pulled back.

"Take a look."

Miles looked at himself in the mirror. He shook his head and frowned.

"This won't do. There's not enough color. I need more. Yes, more. Transfer more, please." He looked at her and smiled.

Cat obliged and kissed him again. And again.

"Oh, by the way, Sir Miles, you don't have to behave anymore. I release you from your obligation to behave."

"Thank god," Miles groaned. He reached for her and put his arm around her. His other hand tangled in her hair. He pulled her tight against him, and he began kissing her with abandon.

After a few minutes of this, the kisses became more passionate. Miles groaned softly.

Cat realized that her body was flooded with heat. She pulled away from him.

"Miles, we need to stop for now," Cat said, "or we'll never make it there. We'll miss the parade. We don't want to miss the mariachi band. We can dance, too."

"Can we transfer more again later?" Miles asked. His words were said in a hopeful tone.

"Yes, of course. We can transfer as much you want. But now, let's join the festivities."

"Wait," Miles said. He found his phone and pulled Cat onto his lap. He took a selfie of them together as dead ghosts. Both were smiling broadly.

* * *

Downtown Bisbee was busy and full of participants in their best finery. The Día de los Muertos celebration was a traditional Mexican holiday to celebrate the passing of loved ones. As the crowd gathered to begin the parade, many people carried posters and banners with photos of their departed loved ones. Messages of love and remembrance were written on the signs. Cat carried a small sign with a photo of her recently-deceased brother Luis.

Miles looked at Luis's photo. Cat and her brother looked very much alike. "I think he knows how much you loved him and how much you miss him," he said.

Cat nodded, tears in her eyes. "I'll go to the cemetery tomorrow and leave marigolds on his grave."

The procession began. The crowd made up of people of all ages wound its way down Tombstone Canyon. Cat saw many people she knew. They greeted each other warmly. Many expressed their condolences for Luis's untimely passing. Even more welcomed Cat home to Bisbee. Miles was pleased to hear these welcomes. He knew that Cat would not be alone when he was gone. She had many childhood friends in Bisbee. He felt sad knowing that he would not be there to see this.

Once they'd reached the center of town, the crowd began to disperse from the more-or-less orderly parade formation. Many shops were open, and people went in and out with purchases. A mariachi band had just begun to play. Cat placed her sign with Luis's photo against one of the buildings.

"Dance with me, Sir Miles," she said, taking his hand. She was smiling.

"Of course, m'lady."

And they danced and danced, tune after tune. Miles would frequently spin Cat in a circle. Her skirt swung out and around, she threw her head back, and she laughed again and again. Miles had never seen her so happy.

The mariachi band, all men dressed in the traditional dark suits with silver trimmings and wide hats, decided to take a break.

"This dancing has made me really thirsty," Cat said.

"There's a little convenience store that's open. I'll get us some bottled water."

"Great idea. Let's wander around a bit. Then later, let's go to Amanda's place and have a drink to celebrate."

"I like that."

They made their way through the crowd to the brightly-lit storefront.

"I'll wait here, Miles," Cat said. "I want to see if I know more people. I'd like to say hi to them all and invite them to the gallery."

"You'll stay right here? Not go anywhere?"

"Yes, definitely. I'll be here when you come out."

But she wasn't. Miles went in the store, purchased a couple of bottles of water, and when he came out, Cat wasn't there.

A sinking feeling came over Miles. The feeling quickly changed into full-on alarm. He knew without a doubt that Cat had been abducted. What an idiot he was! He said he'd stick to her like glue. And then, like an idiot, he left her. Never mind that he left her for only three minutes. He left her. He left her unprotected. And now she was gone.

Focus. Focus. Focus. Miles fought the growing sense of panic. He ran into the street to see if there was any chance he could spot Cat. Nothing.

* * *

Cat was waving at some children passing by when the man came to stand next to her. He was dressed all in black, a dark hoodie pulled up over his head. Cat looked at his face. She recognized Nolan Fuller immediately. She glanced into the store. Miles was handing the clerk some money for the bottled water. He would be out in a minute or less.

Fuller thrust the barrel of a small handgun into her side.

"Scream and I'll shoot you," he growled.

"What do you want?"

"You're coming with me." He grabbed her arm, and when Cat resisted, Fuller jerked her hard toward him.

"Don't resist. If you don't come with me quietly, I'll shoot that boyfriend of yours the second he comes out of the store."

Cat complied. The idea that Miles would get hurt because of her was simply something she couldn't risk. She glanced back and could see Miles heading for the door of the convenience store. Her heart was hammering, and her breath was coming in short, terrified gasps.

Fuller pulled her into the deep shadows at the side of the convenience store. He didn't stop. He wrenched her arm again and jerked her with him along a rough trail behind several houses. Then he turned uphill onto another side street. A few steps more and they were at the bottom of the sixth staircase in the Great Stair Climb.

Cat was much smaller than Fuller, with shorter legs, and keeping up with him was difficult. She kept looking back, but she couldn't see Miles at all. Tears came to her eyes. She was out of breath, and she knew that shortness of breath was going to get worse. The staircase had one hundred thirty steps.

Fuller jerked her closer and began pulling her up the staircase. Rather than turning left toward her house, Fuller turned to the right and pulled her along another road.

Cat realized that he was taking her to his home, empty now because Fuller's wife Helen had fled Bisbee. Would Miles be able to find her? Fear turned to terror.

* * *

Miles stood in the street paralyzed. Cat had been gone only a minute, but he couldn't see her anywhere. She had disappeared into the dark. He was quite certain that Nolan Fuller had taken her. But where?

To Cat's home and gallery? Not likely. Too risky.

To Jax Beringer's home? Freddy Howard had been staying there. Fuller likely knew that. Also, it was too easy to see what was going on there. The neighbor Mary Erik had shown them that.

Fuller's destination had to be his own home. Fuller no doubt knew that his wife was gone. He had the place to himself. No one would think it unusual to see him coming and going, even if it was with a woman dressed in traditional Día de los Muertos costume. Cat would most likely not be recognized.

That had to be it. Where else could he go quickly while dragging a woman with him?

Miles closed his eyes and imagined the map of Bisbee he had studied when readying himself for the Great Stair Climb. Yes, Fuller's house was closest to the sixth staircase, the very one where Cat had been assaulted.

Miles turned and took off running at top speed to the street where the sixth staircase could be found. He mounted the stairs four at a time. When he neared Fuller's house, he paused. Yes, there was the faintest sliver of light showing between closed curtains. He struggled to control his breath so he wouldn't be heard. He approached the back door.

He could hear Cat's voice.

* * *

Only a few minutes earlier, Fuller had opened the door to his house and shoved Cat inside. He turned on a small light.

"Sit down there," he said in a rough voice. He pointed to a wooden chair.

"Why are you doing this?" Cat asked. "What do you want?"

"I want what you've got. I want all of Jax's paintings. I want that big painting, the one he called 'Kissed.'"

Cat released a gush of air. Good god. Jax Beringer was ….she couldn't think of a good word to describe Beringer's narcissism, his willingness to hurt and humiliate people. And Fuller was one of those people who had been hurt. She dare not tell him that she'd already sold the painting to Jessica Cameron.

Fuller sat down in a chair a few feet away, his back to the door. He was still holding the gun, but now it was resting in his hand on his thigh.

"It would have been so easy. If you'd just agreed to sell me the gallery, then I could have legally obtained control not only of the paintings you have, but also that contract your brother signed with him."

Cat frowned. She realized he didn't really understand how all that contract and probate worked. He was assuming that he would get everything.

"Yeah," Fuller continued. His tone was smug. "I know all about the contract. Jax told me about it. I knew then that if I got control of the gallery, then I would take over the contract as well. Whatever he painted would be under my control. I told him this, and he just laughed at me."

"So you killed him?"

"I didn't mean to. I was just so angry. I lost my mind. I picked up the hammer that girl carpenter had left there. I hit him. I couldn't stop hitting him."

"Why did you bring me here?"

"Like I said, you could have sold out to me. But no, you wouldn't even consider it. So I figure if you're gone, then I can be first in line to get your estate. Jax owed me a lot of money, and I can make a claim on the estate. But instead of money, I want the gallery and all the paintings."

"You're pretty sure of yourself." Cat stared at him with her eyes wide open. She looked at his face but in her peripheral vision, she could see the door they'd just come through begin to open slowly. She wanted to keep Fuller distracted.

"I have a plan for you," he sneered.

"What's that?"

"I'm going to eliminate you. I'll make it easy on you by shooting you in the head. It will be easier and faster than that hammer. Then I'm going to slice you open just like I did Jax."

"And put me in the wall?" Cat blinked. The door was open far enough to see who was on the other side. Miles Trevelyan. Tears came to her eyes.

"Yes, as a matter of fact." Fuller laughed a short, humorless laugh. "But instead of the gallery, I'm going to put you in this wall. The wall of my own home. My wife has abandoned me so I'll be the only one here, waiting for the probate process to complete. Then I'll move into your place above the gallery when I take control. Perhaps I'll burn this house to the ground. What's left of you will go up in flames." He laughed again at his own cruel joke.

Cat shook her head. The phrase "ruthless homicidal maniac" was all she could think.

Miles was inside now. Cat saw him reach for Mari Spencer's hammer which was on a small table near the door.

Without thinking, she stood.

Fuller lunged for her, and when he did, the gun fell to the floor. As he lunged, he pulled a thin-bladed, very sharp boning knife from a sheath at the small of his back. He pushed Cat's body away while holding onto one of her wrists. The sharp blade in his hand found Cat's forearm. Immediately her blood began flowing from the cut, emerging as a red line from elbow to wrist.

Miles must have made some small sound because Fuller grew suddenly stiff. He jerked his body around toward the door. Before he could move to attack, Miles hit Fuller's head with a hard but glancing blow of the hammer, just enough to knock him out. Fuller fell onto the floor, unconscious.

"Oh, Miles," Cat gasped. She threw herself across the room and into his arms.

"Are you okay?" Miles held her close. His heart was beating wildly, as was Cat's. "No, you're not okay. Let me see what he did to your arm."

He looked closely. "We need to get you to the hospital. You're bleeding."

"Did you hear what he said he was going to do to me?"

Miles nodded. "I did. I had to stop him. I didn't hit him very hard, though. I didn't want to kill him, just knock him out."

"You saved my life."

Miles let her go.

"Let's find something to tie him up because he's going to regain consciousness soon," he said.

"I'll call Sam." Her arm was hurting, and blood was dripping from the open wound. She found her phone.

Miles searched until he found some rope. He tied Fuller's hands behind his back. Then Miles looped the ends of rope around Fuller's bent legs and ankles. The effect was to tighten the rope if Fuller pulled on it at all.

Cat connected with Sam Morales. The call was brief. They disconnected.

Miles took Cat into the bathroom, found a towel and wrapped it around her arm.

Ten minutes later, Bisbee Police Chief Sam Morales and two deputies from the Cochise County's Sheriff's Department arrived. They hauled Fuller away.

One of the deputies dropped Cat and Miles at her home. Miles put her immediately into his car, and they went to the emergency room at the hospital in Bisbee's Warren district.

They got in to see a doctor right away. He cleaned away the blood with antiseptic. Then he applied butterfly bandages along the length of her arm except where the deepest part of the cut required a couple of stitches. The nurse gave Cat an injection of antibiotics.

"Not so bad, not so bad," the doctor said repeatedly. "This is going to hurt for a couple of days. But the wound isn't deep. This could have been a lot worse. This cut didn't hit a vein. That could have caused major bleeding. So I'm letting you go. Come back if you have any sign of infection. Take your antibiotic pills."

Cat nodded. Her arm hurt. Really hurt.

"It hurts," she said.

The doctor gave her a second injection to relieve pain. He looked at Miles. "Take her home and keep her quiet."

Miles nodded.

Cat and Miles spoke very little on their drive home from the hospital. There they went directly to Cat's room. Miles removed Cat's shoes, then his. Together they lay down on Cat's bed. Miles covered them both with a blanket. He pulled Cat into his arms under the blanket. They held each other until they fell asleep wrapped in each other's arms.

16 Cat and Miles

Cat's wound began to heal quickly. She and Miles spent some time working on the art inventory. They said little to each other. He wandered off on his own, usually in the afternoon.

Cat watched Miles go up the hill as if he were off on a hike along the trail above Bisbee. She didn't know what to say to him. He was leaving shortly. And he apparently didn't know what to say to her. His eyes were sad when he looked at her.

Later, Amanda would tell her that he had gone directly to the Star Tavern each day. He sipped his stout and looked miserable the entire time.

On the night before Miles was scheduled to leave, he and Cat ate together in her kitchen. After dinner, he handed her a card in an envelope.

"I wanted to give you a gift, but I couldn't think of anything that seemed right. So here's a card. It has one of my very favorite Rumi quotations."

Cat pulled the card from the envelope. There was that selfie photo of her with Miles in their Día de los Muertos costumes and makeup. Both were smiling broadly. She opened the card. Inside there was a beautiful hand-calligraphed poem. It read:

Run from what's comfortable.
Forget safety.
Live where you fear to live.
Destroy your reputation.
Be notorious.

"Are you familiar with Rumi?" Miles asked.

"He was a Persian poet. I took a world lit class in college." Cat looked at him. "This calligraphy is lovely."

"Thank you."

"You did this? It's really very good."

Miles reached out and took her hand in his. "Doing calligraphy is very meditative. I really like it."

Cat was quiet. She stared at their entwined hands.

"Rumi was right," she finally said. She stood up.

"Come on, Miles. Come with me." She pulled him as fast as she could from his chair and then up the stairs into her bedroom. She closed the door behind them.

"That's my bed," Cat said to Miles. She gestured to the bed.

He nodded, smiling.

Cat reached down and pulled back the top layer of covers. She looked at him.

"That's my bed."

He raised his eyebrows and cocked his head.

Cat took both his hands in hers. "Miles?"

"Yes, m'lady."

"I was wondering if you'd do me a favor before you go."

"Anything."

"Will you please make love with me?" she said in an unsure voice.

Miles smiled. "I'd be honored, m'lady. Honored." He pulled Cat into his arms.

* * *

Cat woke the next morning feeling better than she'd ever felt in her entire life. She stretched and yawned. Then she sank back against her pillow. Her thoughts were of Miles. She reached out for him in her bed. Nothing. He wasn't there. Suddenly the awareness that this was the day he was leaving hit her in the chest and in her heart. Her eyes filled with tears.

Cat could hear noise in the kitchen below. Miles was tinkering around, making coffee and maybe even breakfast. She rose, threw on a robe and went to the bathroom for a quick shower.

Miles found her on the outdoor deck sitting in the morning sun. Cat had a pair of sunglasses perched on her head.

"Good morning, m'lady. Care for a coffee?"

He set a tray with two coffees on the table.

"Thank you, Miles."

He sat next to her and began sipping his coffee.

The morning was lovely, an autumn morning full of sunshine. Miles looked down Tombstone Canyon. The town was just beginning to wake up. He thought this must be the loveliest place in the world, and he was sitting next to the loveliest woman he'd ever known. His heart was filled with love for her.

"Cat," he began.

She glanced at him and then looked away.

Miles frowned. "This is killing me," he muttered.

She nodded. "We knew it would end this way."

"I'm going to do my best to make sure it doesn't end."

Cat looked at him. His face was open, sad and resigned at the same time.

"You are an incredibly good lover. You're kind and sweet and funny, and you rescued me from a killer. I can't expect or ask for more than that. It's been great being with you. But let's face it. I knew from day one that you were leaving. You have a whole other life in England. I never expected you to drop everything and stay here with me. I'm letting you go, Sir Miles."

He grimaced. "But Cat…"

Before he could say anything else, she said, "Miles, go. Go now before I start crying because if I start, I won't be able to stop." She paused and looked at him. "*Vaya con Dios, mi amor.*" Go with God, my love. She slipped the sunglasses down over her eyes and turned her face away from him.

Miles hesitated. He sighed, put the coffee cup down, and reached out to touch her shoulder. He rose and walked away.

Cat heard him close the back door. A few minutes later, Miles drove away toward the west on Tombstone Canyon Road.

* * *

Seven weeks passed. The winter solstice was coming in just a couple of days. Cat had done her best to stay as busy as possible in the weeks since Miles had gone away. He had texted her a few times. His messages were brief. They gave her an update on what he was doing, and always ended with "I miss you." She responded in kind. She figured that the texts would become fewer and farther between until they stopped completely. She really never expected to see him again.

She was busy sweeping the floor of the gallery when her phone chimed. She looked at the text on her phone, grinned, and texted back, "Yes! Give me five minutes."

Cat rushed to the front door of the gallery and flipped the "Out to Lunch-Back at 1 pm" sign over, even though it was only nine in the morning and a Sunday. She rushed to the staircase and took the stairs two at a time up to her newly redesigned sitting room-office. Opening her laptop, Cat turned it on and waited impatiently for it to load everything. It didn't take long, but it seemed to take forever. She clicked on Skype and connected. There he was, grinning at her. Miles Trevelyan. It seemed like so very long since she'd seen his handsome face.

"Hi! *Hola!*"

"Hello, m'lady. How are you?"

"Great! And how's my favorite baronet?"

He laughed. "Your favorite? I'm the only baronet you know."

"Yeah, so what? You're still my favorite."

"It's nine in the morning there? I wanted to make sure I was able to connect with you in your morning. It's four in the afternoon here."

Cat nodded. "I was sweeping up downstairs."

"What's going on in the great metropolis of Bisbee, Arizona?"

"Well, you'll be interested to know that the authorities had to haul Nolan Fuller off to a facility for the criminally insane. He'll be tried whenever they can get enough meds in him so he can understand what's happening. Sam Morales told me that Fuller has been incoherent. Sam says he attacks anyone who comes near him."

"Lost his mind, then?"

"Yep, batshit crazy."

Miles shook his head. "What else is going on there?"

"We had the grand opening of the gallery last night. Tons of people came. They drank up all my wine and bought about three thousand dollars' worth of art. Mostly small stuff."

"Excellent. I had this feeling that you would do really well."

"I've been over to the house next door, the one Luis left me in his will. The tenants are in the process of moving out."

"Yes? And you'll move in?"

"I'm thinking I will. The house is huge. All on one level."

"No need for a lift then."

"No need for an elevator." Cat smiled at him.

Miles laughed.

"The house has four bedrooms, a big dining room and an even bigger living room. The kitchen is huge. The backyard is fenced, and there's room for a garden, too. If I move in, I might adopt a rescue dog."

Cat could see that Miles had a look of genuine pleasure on his face.

"Good idea. Get a big dog, one that can take care of you."

"How about you? What are you doing these days? How's the weather in jolly old England? How's your dad?"

"Oh, as one would expect for mid-December. Cold and rainy. It's already snowed a couple of times, too. My dad's fine. He said to say hi. I've been teaching a seminar, but that will soon be over. I'm making an effort to make sense of all the notes I made when I was traveling on the border. I talked to an editor at Oxford University Press. He's interested in my book. I just have to focus and write it."

"You can do it, Miles."

"I seem to have trouble concentrating." He frowned. "Anything else new? Any new friends?"

New friends? What does that mean? Cat frowned in confusion.

"No, same friends," she said. "Actually, I do have a new friend. My cousin. Or second cousin. Whatever. I'm forming sort of a friendship with my cousin Frankie. He's really smart and funny. He came over for a visit a week or so ago. I'm becoming friends with some of the artists and other business owners here, too. I spend a fair amount of time with Amanda. You remember her from the Star Tavern? She's a little older than me, but she doesn't seem to mind, nor do I. That's about it for new friends."

"Good. Frankie's a nice fellow. And Amanda is a good person, too. And her ales and stouts are wonderful. And with Amanda, you'll always know what's going on in Bisbee."

"The lawyer Jessica Cameron has been back here. She's really well organized. The probate process is up and running now. Jessica is especially interested in seeing Carmen Fuentes get child support for her baby. Also I shipped that painting to her in Tucson. 'Kissed' is gone, gone, gone."

Cat paused. She suddenly realized what Miles had been thinking about when he asked if she had any new friends. He wanted to know if she had a new love interest.

"Are you trying to find out if I have a new boyfriend?"

"That obvious, huh?"

"No, no one new. I had a boyfriend, but he got on an airplane and flew away. I cried all day when he left. I cried the next day, too. I still cry when I think of him because I miss him so much. I hope he comes back someday."

Miles nodded. He frowned. His mouth was in a tight line.

"I'm sorry I made you cry."

Cat nodded. Time to change the subject or she'd start crying again.

"I have this feeling that something is going on with you. What is it?" she asked.

"Well, I was thinking my concentration might improve if I had a change of scenery over the holidays. I have almost a month free. I was thinking of someplace warm and sunny with good burritos and stout and maybe a margarita from time to time."

Cat laughed. "I know just the place. Buy your air tickets, give me your arrival date and time, and I'll pick you up at the Tucson airport."

"Thanks, but I really like the idea of renting a car and driving for a couple of hours through the desert. I've missed the desert. I want to drive through Benson and St. David and Tombstone, and then arrive in Bisbee."

"I'll be here."

"That's okay with you? I can stay with you?"

"More than okay. Of course you can stay with me. You *must* stay with me. You don't know how much I've missed you."

"And I've missed you. You're often in my thoughts, m'lady. Every day."

"There's only one problem."

"What's that?" He looked a little worried.

"I turned my brother's old bedroom into a little sitting room and office. So there's no bed in that room anymore. As you know, I sleep in the other bedroom." She grinned. She couldn't help but tease him a little.

"So where will I sleep?" He was grinning, too.

"You'll have to share the bed with me. My bed is small so we'll have to sleep really close together."

"Really close? I quite like that idea. Your wish is my command, m'lady."

They sat staring and smiling at each other over Skype.

Then his demeanor changed completely. Miles frowned and looked very serious.

"I have something else to tell you."

"Bad news?" Cat felt suddenly anxious.

"Actually, I hope you'll consider it good news. I'm a little fearful about telling you. Maybe you won't think it's good news at all. I'll be really disappointed if that happens."

"Go on. What is it?"

"I didn't tell you about this because I didn't know how it would turn out, and I didn't want to disappoint you. But when I was in Tucson, I went in for an interview at the University of Arizona. One of my colleagues there recommended me for a teaching position. I just heard from the faculty rep. They found funding to hire me, and they've offered me a job starting next autumn. They'll arrange for me to get a green card when I arrive so I'll be legal. I'll be an assistant professor at the university."

Cat burst into tears. Her hands were clasped in front of her chest.

"Oh!" Miles said in dismay.

"Tears of joy!" she sobbed.

He grinned. "Thank god. I didn't know if you would want me around that much. I was afraid that I might be just a holiday romance to you, and you would forget me."

"You're *loco*."

"I'll keep an apartment in Tucson, but I can visit you on weekends and holidays. And you can visit me in Tucson."

"That's the best news I've ever had in my whole entire life ever," Cat sobbed.

"Then stop crying," he laughed.

"I'm not crying," she sniveled. "I'm expressing."

"Of course you are. I wish I could hold you right now," he said tenderly. "I won't be there in the spring except maybe for a week's mid-term vacation, but I could actually move to Arizona next summer. In June."

"You may change your mind completely if you come here in the summer. It gets a bit warm here."

"I've been in Arizona before in the summer. I can handle it. Plus it won't be so hot in Bisbee."

"True."

"Although it may get hot in your bed."

Cat giggled.

"Look. I know we didn't know each other very long, but I have a special feeling about you and me…..together, I mean," Miles said.

Cat nodded. "I have a special feeling about you and me, too."

"So I'm hoping that when I move to Tucson, we'll be able to spend more time with each other. We can really get to know each other. Maybe this thing between us will turn into something…."

"Yeah, something…." Cat was smiling now. "Something more than lust?"

Miles laughed. "Yes, something more, but we don't want to give up the lust."

"Never," smiled Cat. "I feel a lot of lust for you. You are a very sexy man."

Miles turned pink.

"Oh, Sir Miles is blushing," Cat laughed.

They stared at each other, both smiling.

"Got to go," he finally said. "I'll send you my travel plans. I'm looking forward to seeing you in the same spot you were in when I left — sitting in the sun on your deck reading a book and drinking coffee or maybe a margarita."

"I'll be on the deck waiting for you. I've really missed you."

"Not as much as I've missed you," Miles said.

"So it's not just the sun and the margaritas that make you want to return?"

"No. You first. Then the sunny desert days and the starry desert nights and the margaritas and the burritos and the mariachi music and you. You first and you last."

"You're so sweet."

"*Ya me voy*," Miles said. I'm going now.

Cat blew him a kiss. "*Hasta pronto, mi amor.*" See you soon, my love.

Thank you from the Author:

Hello Reader! Thank you for reading *Kissed,* the first Cat Miranda Mystery. I hope you enjoyed accompanying Cat and Miles on all their adventures. Please leave a review of this book on your favorite book vendor website. By leaving a review for others to read, you can make it much easier for mystery readers everywhere to find this book. Thank you so much. A new Cat Miranda Mystery is being written now. Also don't forget Letty Valdez. The fourth Letty Valdez Mystery is coming soon. To learn more, go to www.cjshane.com, sign up for my monthly newsletter, and feel free to email me with comments or questions.

About the Author:

C.J. Shane is a writer and visual artist based in Tucson, Arizona, U.S.A. She has traveled widely and lived and worked in Mexico, the People's Republic of China, and in the U.S. She has worked as a newspaper reporter, freelance writer, academic reference librarian, and ESL teacher. She is the author of eight nonfiction books. Her first work of fiction, *Desert Jade: A Letty Valdez Mystery* (2017) was a finalist for Best Thriller Suspense, New Mexico-Arizona Book Awards, and *Dragon's Revenge: A Letty Valdez Mystery* (2018), a finalist for Best Mystery and Best Multicultural Work, NM-AZ Book Awards. The third Letty Valdez Mystery, *Daemon Waters,* was published late in 2019. See more at www.cjshane.com or www.RopesEndPublishing.com